PRAISE FOR THE NOVELS OF ANNE RIVERS SIDDONS

THE GIRLS OF AUGUST

"This novel illustrates the beautiful and startling ways friendships remain and evolve over times. Reading it will help you remember who your real friends are."
—*The Daily Beast*

"[A] great combination of Southern gothic and emotional realism."
—*Columbus Dispatch (OH)*

"Majestic...[Siddons] has a way with words, and the natural flow of her narrative makes it easy to get lost in the lives of four women, as they persevere through two decades of joy, sadness and hope."
—*Bookreporter.com*

BURNT MOUNTAIN

"Atmospheric...exciting...a master storyteller with a remarkable track record."
—*Booklist*

The Girls of

August

The Girls of August

ANNE RIVERS SIDDONS

GRAND CENTRAL
PUBLISHING

NEW YORK   BOSTON

Copyright © 2014 by Anne Rivers Siddons

Cover photography by Cig Harvey
Cover design by Catherine Casalino
Cover copyright © 2016 by Hachette Book Group, Inc.

Grand Central Publishing
Hachette Book Group
1290 Avenue of the Americas
New York, NY 10104
grandcentralpublishing.com
twitter.com/grandcentralpub

Originally published in hardcover and ebook by Grand Central Publishing in July 2014.
First Mass Market Edition: July 2016

Grand Central Publishing is a division of Hachette Book Group, Inc.
The Grand Central Publishing name and logo is a trademark of Hachette Book Group, Inc.

The publisher is not responsible for websites (or their content) that are not owned by the publisher.

The Hachette Speakers Bureau provides a wide range of authors for speaking events. To find out more, go to www.hachettespeakersbureau.com or call (866) 376-6591.

ISBN: 978-0-446-61823-6 (mass market); 978-0-446-56584-4 (ebook)

Printed in the United States of America

OPM

10 9 8 7 6 5 4 3 2 1

To Allyson, with dearest love

The *Girls* of

August

Prologue

Of all the fifteen summerhouses, the first one was the best. That's what we all agreed on, for a while, anyway...until we grew wiser, more measured in our joy, more careful with the doling out of praise. Funny, we rarely agreed unanimously on anything, but for years there had been no doubt about the Colleton house. At first glance it had seemed designed— brick, board, and shingle—for the girls of August.

A silly name for four women who, after a decade and a half of never missing an August together, were approaching middle age, fretting over crow's-feet, and reaching for skin cream. It had seemed silly to us even when we were in our twenties, when one of our husbands—had it been Mac or Oliver? No one could remember—coined it, the first summer we'd taken a beach house together, back when our men were still residents in med school. We were not girls even then. Strictly speaking, I don't think some of us ever were.

But it had been August. And somehow, after that first time, it always was.

Odd how that week—the second week to be exact because it gave us time to breathe before school and fall and the holidays—had cemented itself into our lives.

"It's like Christmas, or goddamned New Year," Mac had said once, when we had been invited by his friends the Copleys to spend the first two weeks in August aboard their yacht, the *Spindrift*, cruising from Savannah to the Bahamas and back.

"Why the hell can't y'all just move it forward or back? I'll never get another chance to fish for a solid ten days." He blinked his eyes, a sure sign—I had come to learn over the years—of his being desperate to have his way.

"We just can't," I said, knowing not why, only that we couldn't. It felt to each of the girls of August as if the universe would tilt on its axis and no one would be the same if we adjusted the timing of our yearly gathering. "That's just when it is. We've already rented the house. Go fishing with the Copleys, by all means. I'll bet La Serenissima has a dozen itsy-bitsy teeny-weeny bikinis."

Mac snorted. Serena Copley in a bikini would have been as ludicrous as a hippo in a wet suit. She was not fat, but at six feet and with shoulders as wide as a linebacker's, she packed more muscle than Arnold Schwarzenegger. She was, as her dandelion-frail husband, Dave, said frequently, every inch an athlete.

"She could easily tow the boat in her teeth," Mac groused. But he went fishing and I went, happily, to the Gulf Coast of Alabama.

In the early days, we always chose a spot along the northern Gulf Coast because it was within shouting distance of Nashville and Vanderbilt's med school, where, as Rachel was fond of saying, we were all stationed, as if life in med school were akin to military service. Given the long hours residents kept and the often life-or-death decisions they had to make, her military allusion bore some merit.

But back to that first trip, taken in haste—almost hysteria—because the girls had wanted, I suppose, to claim time as fiercely as our men did. Beautiful Point Clear, Alabama. The house had belonged to Teddy's first wife, Cornelia, who would ultimately leave Teddy, a few months after he went into private practice, for a college boyfriend whose family boasted as much money as her own, taking her wonderful beach house with her.

Let me be clear. We did not mourn Cornelia. I don't think even Teddy did. She was a lazy, drawling aristocrat whose sole persona seemed to be heavy-lidded amusement at the likes of the rest of us. But for a good long while we sorely missed her rambling gray-shingled beach house with its endless airy rooms reminiscent of a Ralph Lauren ad, surrounded by a picket fence drooling *Rosa rugosa* and dipping its feet into the warm green sea.

We all took turns finding the next August's beach house, but we perpetually complained that none were as *House Beautiful*–perfect as the Colletons'. Perhaps our affection for the place was like a first love. It takes the long view of history to snuff out the glow.

"Old Mobile money, you know," Teddy had said asininely when he first introduced his rich golden girl to the rest of the group. I, unfortunately, had already met her, but that is another story. She officially came into the group fold, as it were, on Mac's birthday. I'd cobbled together enough champagne and crepe paper to throw him a proper party in our cramped apartment that was within walking distance of the hospital.

"How nice for you," I'd purred to Teddy. None of us had much money; the guys, of course, were still residents. The idea of their finding practices to join, or trying to start their own, was nothing but a distant dream. Only Mac and I were married then, newly-weds full of blush and blather, though Rachel and Barbara were very much in the picture. Their weddings to Oliver and Hugh followed soon after ours.

"Madison, dear, don't worry. We'll wait till the fuss about yours dies down," Cornelia had said silkily just after our wedding, a champagne glass sparkling in her exquisitely manicured, alabaster hand. "I'd hate for Teddy's and mine to be upstaged by the memory."

"Yeah, right," Rachel had whispered in my ear in her froggy New Jersey voice as she made her way to the canapés, which I'd made myself, sacrificing sleep but gaining pride. "You wait," Rachel growled. "Hers will upstage Di and Charles's."

And in many ways, I thought that it had. Their wedding was held on a late spring day on the lush emerald lawn of the house on Point Clear, against the backdrop of rioting *Rosa rugosa* and green waves curling onto pearl-white sand, with eight bridesmaids (none of us among them) dressed in billowing blue tulle and Cornelia herself in layers of diaphanous white silk that blew in the rose-scented wind like the petals of a flower.

Teddy, startling in a cutaway and wickedly starched collar, looked as if the wind might pick him up and whirl him into Mobile Bay. He was so pale that his relentless five-o'clock shadow stood out like a pirate's beard, although I was sure he had shaved hardly an hour before. He seemed tossed like flotsam in the sea of silks and satins and flowers and wondrous, huge-brimmed hats that surged around him.

I stood with Rachel and Barbara—our men were Teddy's groomsmen—and realized that I had seldom seen him in anything but green scrubs. This, sadly, was not an improvement.

But oh, the house! That wonderful, wind-riding, sea-drinking house! When it became clear that our group, which was surviving the rigors of med school thanks to inky coffee and catnaps stolen on the fly, would inevitably be blown asunder by the advent of far-flung job opportunities—no more Nashville, no more "I'll be right over" when one of us was in crisis—Rachel, Barbara, and I had determined that a week-long getaway, possibly a yearly one, was in order. The men's residency schedules, we knew, would eventually be overtaken by careers and the detritus of life. So one late Friday night, as we chatted around a table cluttered with empty wine bottles, we insisted that no matter where the future took us, we would reserve one week for ourselves.

"Always and forever," I had said.

"Hear, hear!" Barbara and Rachel had chimed in in unison, and to seal the deal, we clinked glasses.

Cornelia, who, in addition to being transparently beautiful in the way of fair-headed blondes, was inordinately nosy, caught on to our harried plan in nothing flat. Not to be left out, she offered her summerhouse for free. Of course, that meant she would join us. But we could handle that. We could deal with her old-money mannerisms and, we naïvely thought, perhaps make her a better woman.

Sadly, the Colleton house—as soon as we laid eyes on it—became the standard by which we judged all the subsequent getaway houses. Under the spell snobbery sometimes casts, we would find a perfectly lovely summer home and spend much of our week carping that it wasn't as pitch-perfect as Cornelia's. Even though some were warm and happy houses (and some, frankly, dreadful, like the one on the Outer Banks that had oil drums and a defunct gas pump behind it), Cornelia's home stalked our imaginations like a lion in the veldt.

However, its perch among the rugosas and on the sweet warm Gulf fortunately gave rise to a rigid criterion that did serve us well: Whatever house we would choose in the future, it had to be isolated and on the oceanfront.

Years later—after it became clear that some of us were cursed with empty wombs and some of us had to work harder than others to keep our marriages afloat—it dawned on me that I had not really liked that house. Not really. Rather, it had seemed like a duty to like it, and I could not put my finger on the reasons why.

I tried to explain it one afternoon to the *real* girls of August. Yes, the *real* girls. Cornelia had long since decamped with her old-Mobile-money scion (she'd lasted only a single season), and Teddy, within the year, had brought Melinda into our circle.

Melinda Marshall-soon-to-be-Patterson promptly made up for a hundred imperfect beach houses. She was, down to her marrow, genuine and funny and smart. We welcomed her with the unbridled satisfaction that often accompanies the phrase *out with the old and in with the new*. Yes. Simply put, Teddy did himself and us a big favor when he married Melinda.

So there we were—not knowing it was the last time the four of us would be together—lolling about on the grand porch of a weather-beaten charmer in St. Teresa, Florida, drinking margaritas and gazing at the languorous Gulf.

"That house just seemed to have way too many gewgaws... bibelots, I think Cornelia called them... simply too much... no chance to rest your eyes," I said.

"If you looked at all that expensive crap the wrong way it would break. What the hell was wrong with us? Why have we spent so many years admiring a glass house when we should have been throwing stones?" Rachel chimed in, rolling her blue eyes.

"Cornelia!" Barbara spit in her clear, precise schoolteacher's voice, flicking a mosquito off her wrist.

"Right." Rachel bobbed her head in agreement. "Snotty little bitch."

"The oil cans and gas pump were better," I said, swirling my glass, the clinking of ice underscoring my certainty.

"Pity I never met her," Melinda murmured, staring out to sea, and I believe she meant it.

Melinda, of the heavy coiled mahogany mane and aquamarine eyes and the smattering of copper freckles across her nose, the only real beauty among us. Melinda, of the laugh that rang like shattered Lalique and the tongue that could bite like a copperhead. Melinda, of the joyous heart that held us all like a mother's hand. Oh, Melinda...for so long it was Madison and Rachel and Barbara and Melinda, we four, the original girls of August, for Cornelia never truly counted. How we loved Melinda! How, the very moment Teddy brought her into our lives, we all said, "Yes!"

And then, after fifteen summers, Melinda was gone, killed in a car crash on an icy, rutted Kentucky back road far, far, far from the sea. Teddy had been at the wheel. They'd gone to look at a horse he had planned on buying her. A Christmas present. Melinda, like me, was unable to have children, so to fill up that lonely space in her life, they had decided that her love for dogs, cats, horses, and anything else that walked on four legs should be sated with the acquisition of a prize filly. After leaving Rolling Hills Stable, to celebrate the intended purchase, they'd stopped at an inn and eaten dinner. I'm sure Teddy had his requisite three scotches. The bitch in me feels absolutely, stone-eyed certain of that.

Black ice is a killer, you know. And so is disregard for how quickly a happy life can be snuffed out, especially in bad weather when you take a curve too fast.

He didn't see the ice, of course, but he should have known it was there. As they sped toward home, the car spun out on the slick surface and he couldn't regain control. Going sixty miles an hour, they slammed into a tree.

Teddy was basically unhurt. The love of his life was dead. I do not know what that must have been like for Teddy. He was a doctor, for Christ's sake, and he could not save his own wife.

And though the tragedy was deemed an accident, I think we all quietly seethed. *If only, if only, if only...*

So then we were down to three again: Madison McCauley and Rachel Greene and Barbara Fowler, women long past girlhood who were married to physicians practicing in cities across the South, linked by nothing more than the memories of fifteen houses on fifteen beaches in fifteen vanished Augusts.

We exchanged Christmas cards, but the long phone conversations gradually ended, as did the letters and e-mails. It was as though, after all these years, the only thing that bound us together was the memory of Melinda. But we couldn't deal with that. Her absence was as alive and painful as her presence had been alive and joyful.

When she was gone, there was no replacement. Period.

Wind whistled in my heart during those few years after Melinda's death. I think it did in the hearts of Barbara and Rachel too. We were lost. And besides, there could not be only three girls of August. The set was four, even if that came into being only through Cornelia's selfish insistence.

So we stopped gathering.

*   *   *

"I can't imagine having friends that long," my niece Curry said to me during her last visit before she departed for the North and her first semester at Harvard. She was moving to Cambridge over the summer so she could get *acclimated*. She kept saying the word, as if trying it on, sometimes uttering it in a truly terrible bid at a Boston accent.

Curry was almost my own child. She was, in fact, Mac's sister's child, but Charlotte worked long hours and was often out of town, and Curry came to us as naturally as the air we breathed. It wasn't unusual for her to stay with us for several weeks, even a month or so. By that day when we sat on the guest room bed, which had long ago become known as Curry's bed, talking of friends and men, I thought of her as my own. Charlotte never seemed to mind. And when

I looked into her daughter's bright blue eyes, I saw Mac, and I sometimes imagined that she really was our child. But then I stopped, because the longing hurt too much.

I did not know in whom the barrenness lay. Mac? Or me? And Mac was adamant that we not attempt to find out. "No one person to blame," he said.

Melinda supported Mac's viewpoint that we should not know. And even though Teddy and Melinda had been in the same boat as Mac and me, our twin situations gave me no comfort.

Month after month went by and I grew ever more desperate because the pee stick test—no matter how hard I willed otherwise—remained negative. When I'd had enough hurt, when the pain of not having a child grew unbearable, I lobbied for us to go to a fertility clinic.

But Mac stood firm. "There is no guarantee it will work. It can wreck your health, Maddy. And I don't want either of us at any time to look at the other and think, 'If it hadn't been for you . . .' That's a marriage killer, Maddy. Let it lie."

And so, after a good long while, I gave up. Oh, I had deep aches for my unborn many times, and I suppose Mac did too. But I alone had felt I would die of it. Our cure? We both sank deeply into our work, me first as an elementary school teacher and then as the busy owner of my own catering firm, and Mac as a deeply dedicated family physician. We worked and we worked because it was the right thing to do. Sometimes it even kept our pain at bay.

And of course there was Curry...

*　　　*　　　*

"Well, honey, of course you don't know what it would be like to have friends as long as Barbara, Rachel, and I have been together, because you're only eighteen," I said to Curry that morning in her bedroom. I was being artificially cheerful because, though I was pleased as punch that she was going to Harvard, I also didn't want her to leave.

"But you've known each other for twenty years. Maybe more. That's like being married or something," she said, slipping her hand into mine.

"Well, you know we haven't seen each other in three years, not since Melinda..." I trailed off and with my free hand traced a bloom on the magnolia-patterned spread. "I sometimes wonder if we're friends at all anymore."

In the past two weeks, in our usual bent toward haste, Barbara, Rachel, and I had decided—after a flurry of e-mails had turned into a blizzard—that in the wake of Teddy's new marriage, we would reprise the girls of August.

But sitting there with Curry, holding her hand and

remembering Melinda, I wasn't sure it was such a good idea. Three years is a long time. And we were falling into the old habit of allowing Teddy's latest wife to enter our circle. None of us had even met her because none of us had been invited to the wedding.

"Friends don't stop being friends," Curry said, "just because one of you isn't around anymore." She said this with the authority of a much older woman and my heart broke open in a rush of fresh love for her.

"I don't know, honey. We've barely spoken since the funeral. And we don't know this new wife. What will we even talk about?"

"What did you used to talk about?"

"Oh, what we did together after we met," I said, "and the guys. Of course we talked about our guys." I couldn't tell her that we talked about sex. She, being of an age at which it was impossible to think of "old people" having sex, probably wouldn't have even believed me.

"Well, yeah, Uncle Mac... I can't imagine talking a solid week about him."

"He wasn't always just Uncle Mac, you know," I said, smoothing back the unkempt straw-colored hair that was her uncle's off her forehead. "He was many things you'll never know about, back then. Now too. And besides, what makes you think he was the only guy I had?"

"Oh, tell!" Curry squealed, throwing her long arms around my neck and pulling me toward her just as the sound of raindrops pinged, fat and cold, against the beautiful prismed panes of our old house on Church Street Charleston.

"Not on your very young life," I said around a sudden and surprising lump in my throat. "Even aunts are entitled to a little mystery."

I gazed out the rain-splattered window as I rested in Curry's embrace, and an odd heaviness seized my heart. Yes, a little mystery . . .

CHAPTER

1

The girls of August had decided, given our long hiatus and the introduction of a new person—Baby Gaillard *née* LucyAnne Gaillard, to be exact—that we had best meet ahead of time at my house to map out our strategy and make sure we all felt OK about Tiger Island. We were to meet the second weekend of June, so we had plenty of time to reconnoiter if need be.

I stood in my kitchen, barefoot, anxious, muddling the sugar and mint that would spice the pitcher of mojitos I intended to ply the girls with. They would be arriving momentarily, thus my nerves. Had we changed too much? Had three years been kind or cruel? What if one of us had gotten wildly fat or depressed or mean-spirited? Why, on earth, was I fretting so?

"Calm down," I whispered.

I began juicing the limes. The aroma of citrus and sugar curled through the air, and as I breathed in the tart sweet, I considered our different fates.

Me? I had married a man who would become—in terms of the medical establishment—the least of them: a family practitioner. But in terms of the heart, he towered over Oliver and Hugh and Teddy. Which isn't to say I didn't love and admire the other guys. But I got lucky with Mac. He was, as Curry was so fond of saying, a keeper. I tore off another handful of mint leaves, added them to my stone mortar, and thought how ironic it was that a man who had dedicated his life to healthy families had no children of his own.

As for me, after I quit teaching, I did nothing to serve that relentless baby need—no charity work with homeless or orphaned children, no more volunteer work at the hospital. The lack of kids in my life had made it too painful to be around other people's kids. Maybe that was selfish. But we all have coping mechanisms, and avoiding the sweet voices of the young was my way. So I stayed busy with my catering business and was, in fact, something of a celebrity in old Charleston. And no one suspected that the yearly anonymous donation that kept the School for Children afloat came from Mac and me.

Then there was Rachel's husband, Oliver, who was

one of Atlanta's most esteemed oncologists. The money had changed Oliver, if you ask me. It had made him antiseptic, a wee bit arrogant, a tad remote, but done nothing to diminish his million-dollar smile and his doting affection for the Italian greyhounds they bred and showed. Or maybe it wasn't the money. Maybe dealing with so many profoundly sick and dying people had caused Oliver to lose some of that boyish charm and retreat into a safer space, a space where he didn't feel the world's sadness quite so acutely. That was something I could understand.

Rachel, however, didn't let anything change her. She was a tough Jewish gal from Hoboken, New Jersey, who had, quite simply, a heart of gold. She was sassy and sarcastic, and suffered no fools. She and Oliver had met while he was just beginning his medical residency and she was finishing up her final semester in nursing school. A pediatric nurse with five children, she seemed to have chosen a profession that would serve her offspring, if not herself.

And then there was sweet Barbara, who'd married Hugh, the heart surgeon in our group. With a booming Birmingham practice (Cornelia Colleton's father was among the patients who called him Doc) and an aptness for society and its galas, he had—five years into his practice—demanded that Barbara quit teaching school in order to raise their three children with the help of an imported English nanny.

"Over my dead body, Dr. Fowler," Barbara had told him. "You might love affectation and fine china, but don't ever forget that we're two poor crackers from Marianna, Florida, who happened to get lucky. I will raise my children myself, thank you very much. And I will live out my days as a working woman."

I poured the cold rum into the Waterford pitcher (yes, I liked nice things too) and Barbara bloomed in my mind's eye—her cola-brown eyes flashing with righteousness as she gave Hugh what for—and my anxieties over their visit began to ease. In fact, as I threw back a wee shot of rum, imagining our laughter and conspiratorial whispers, I decided Rachel and Barbara couldn't arrive soon enough.

*   *   *

"I'm not spending a week on an island with anybody named Baby," Rachel said grumpily, looking at the photograph of the house. "I don't care if it's the most perfect beach house on earth."

I watched Rachel from my spot on the sofa and decided these past three years had been good to her. Her chestnut hair still gleamed and her blue eyes shone with that endless curiosity I so loved about her. And, after five kids and twenty-some years, she'd kept her figure. Tall and buxom, she was what you called a handsome woman.

"Just look. The house is to die for. Puts the Colleton house to shame. But really! Baby?" She shoved the photo at Barbara, who had just arrived from Birmingham and had barely had time to put her luggage down before I stuck a mojito in her hand.

"It just about is. Perfect, I mean," Barbara said, her long, beautiful fingers cupping the photo. "Look at that beach. Look at those roses. Actually, Rachel, it *looks* like the Colleton house, only...I dunno...more lived in, a place you could really get used to." She sighed, as if even the mention of the Colleton house filled her with memories too sweet to bear, and then tossed the photo on the coffee table. "Better Baby than Cornelia Colleton, if you ask me," she said, her eyes widening at the mention of Teddy's ex.

"She has another name," I said. "It's LucyAnne. Two words, but all together. Teddy told me."

"Oh, Teddy." Rachel waved her drink dismissively through the air. "Anybody who'd marry a Baby...," Rachel said, and then looked over at me. "Sorry, Maddy."

Before I had dated and married Mac, I had been with Teddy Patterson for almost a year. It was my first year out of Vanderbilt and his first in his residency at the teaching hospital there. I was a brand-new Pink Lady in the evenings, dispensing everything from chewing gum to cigarettes (those were the old days) to hugs, hoping I was providing some measure of comfort to the sick and grieving after my teaching stint at Harrowbrook Elementary was done for the day. Teddy was just starting his long climb toward becoming a pediatric surgeon. We were totally and groggily in love...I more than he, as it turned out.

"Don't worry about it," I said to Rachel. "It was doomed from the start. Baby pointed that out to me not a week ago."

She and Teddy had spent a few days on Tiger Island at the house in the photo, which was Baby's family's summer home, dating back to the early nineteen hundreds. He'd brought her over for supper so she could meet Mac and me before they headed back to Lexington the following day. They actively engaged in a hard sell. Indeed, both Baby and Teddy seemed desperate for us to use the house for our August outing. I suspected Teddy wanted us to accept Baby into our circle because if we did, he would think we'd forgiven him for the accident.

Rachel delicately picked a strand of rum-scented mint from between her teeth. "What do you mean?"

"Well, I was in the kitchen, putting the final touches on my shrimp and grits, and she followed me in there like the proverbial puppy dog, wearing nothing but a dress so short you could see her coochie if you were willing to look. She helped herself to a shrimp right out of the pot, licked her fingers, wiped them on her thigh, and, laughing merrily, said, 'Well, of course you couldn't have married Teddy. You'd have been Madison Patterson. Can you *imagine*?'"

"Little bitch," Rachel snapped.

"What did you say?" asked Barbara, who, I had noticed, seemed to be settling into a middle-aged spread, something I was fighting with every ounce of my being.

"Nothing. As I've gotten older, I'm not so good with the comebacks." I grabbed a couch pillow and drew it to me, cradling it as if it were a fat baby.

We were silent for a moment. I suppose, each in our own way, we were taking stock of not being twenty-three any longer.

Barbara tossed back the sandy-blonde hair that she'd grown out to past her shoulders and, breaking the silence, said in her lovely north Florida drawl, "So, besides being a little bitch, what's she like?"

I gazed down at my drink and thought a moment. I wanted to be fair. And honest. And true to Melinda. Doing all three was going to be impossible. "Well, let's see. She is very, very, very young."

"How young?" Rachel said, slitting her eyes.

I looked first to Rachel and then to Barbara. "Hang on to your panties, girls."

"Oh, gawd! Please tell me she's not jailbait," Barbara said, her plump face revealing hope and shock.

I took a sip and my time. I admit, I relished the suspense. "Well, almost. I'm not sure exactly. But if I had to guess, I think she's legal in most states but probably won't see her third decade for a good long while."

Rachel harrumphed. "No wonder Teddy didn't invite anyone to the wedding. He's ashamed."

Reaching for a sesame cheese straw, Barbara said, "Now give us the really bad news. How beautiful is she?"

"She's pretty, real pretty. And she's got a great body. Even Mac said so and he hardly ever comments on other women. To me, anyway."

"Brunette?" Rachel cocked her head at me.

"Nope. Long blonde hair, deep-green eyes, pert little nose, great boobs. If she were taller, she'd be a model." I wiped the condensation off my glass with my thumb. "She's a traffic-stopper, I'll tell you that much."

"Teddy!" Barbara spit his name the way she'd spit his first wife's name moments before. "He can be such a jerk."

"And a fiend for pretty blondes."

"If it's any consolation," I said, topping off our drinks, "God gave her all body and no brains."

"He went from beautiful, brilliant, grown-up Melinda to a child with no brains?" Rachel looked indignant, and I thought it was a good thing Teddy was in Lexington and not in this room because Rachel might have given him a finger-wagging what for. "What is he thinking!"

"He's not," Barbara said.

"I don't know. He might be," I said, "but it's not with what's up here." I tapped my skull.

"Yeah...he always did think with his pecker," Rachel said, her slight acquired Atlanta lilt sloshing into her New Jersey tough-girl accent.

"And there's another catch," I said.

"Oh-oh. What's that?" Rachel was just about to wiggle out of this deal. I could see it in her face, which was beginning to harden against the whole idea of Tiger Island.

"It's not a week."

"What! But it's always a week. It has to be that way," Barbara said, setting down her drink.

"Something about the guy they hire to ferry them to and fro. He's not going to be available on the seventh day out."

"Why not? Then let's just hire somebody else." Rachel's practical streak was admirable.

"They say there is nobody else. We're going to be out there for fourteen days."

"A two-week vacation!" By the tenor in Barbara's voice, you would have thought she'd never heard of such a thing.

"It's not what we do," Rachel said.

"I agree. It seems unthinkable. But those are the cards they're dealing."

"Two weeks," Rachel said, tilting her head in that wistful manner that dispelled her toughness.

"Yep," I said, warming to the idea even though a part of me feared the whole universe-tilting-on-its-axis threat. "Just the beach and the sun and"—I held up my mojito—"good drink and food."

"Oh well," Barbara said, picking up the photo and studying it. "What are we complaining about? A longer vacation for free? And it's a great house. I vote we live dangerously and take it."

Then she looked at us, levelly, and I thought I caught a glimpse of Barbara the seventh-grade French teacher. "Besides," she said, with not a hint of a grin, "we can always drown Baby."

*   *   *

And that was that. We were going to Tiger Island, or so I thought until Mac and I got into bed that evening. I snuggled under the sheet and rested my head on his bare shoulder. He smelled slightly of shrimp and vodka and I was caught off guard, as I often was, by how thoroughly I loved this big-hearted, Scots-Irish, six-foot-three, rumple-haired, lanky man.

"It's funny," I said.

"What's that?" he asked, gently gathering my hair into a single swath that cascaded over my breast.

"It's as if no time has passed. I mean, Rachel, Barbara, and I just took up where we left off before Melinda died. Or, actually, before we even met Melinda. Three against one...first Cornelia and now poor little pitiful Baby."

Mac traced my collarbone with his index finger. "Poor little pitiful Baby has enough money to buy Cornelia and then some. Teddy...I tell you what, that man can smell money."

"Yes, and in his case money smells just like trouble."

Mac's laughter sounded more rueful than joyful. He kissed my cheek and remained so close I felt his breath against my skin with each word uttered. "Listen to me, Maddy. Why don't you girls just stay in Charleston? Have a good time here, getting reacquainted. Hell, I'll steer clear."

"Honey, that's not how it works."

"In the first place, I think Baby is a nut case," he said. "I don't see how you could spend an hour with her, much less two weeks. And I don't like the idea of Tiger Island. It's just too wild. The weather is crazy. The animals...I don't even have a good idea of what's out there anymore. Rabid coons, for all we know. Besides, it's too hard to get to from Charleston. What if something happens?"

"Sweetheart"—I cupped his face in my hand—"nothing is going to happen. It never does. And believe me, we can handle Baby." As I spoke, an image of Melinda loomed—insouciant and smart and smacking down that young newcomer with one pointed glance of those startling eyes. "And we like the idea of Tiger Island because there isn't anybody on it, nothing, really, except the house. What could bother us there?"

"Well, number one, it's not empty. There's a small Gullah settlement on the western side."

"Oh, well, Gullahs..."

"Most Gullahs I know are far more substantial than a lot of the people we call friends," Mac snapped.

"I didn't mean they weren't. I just meant they're not likely to want to mingle with three middle-aged white ladies and a baby girl, are they? And by the way, do you know any of Baby's people? Seems you would, given that both your families have houses out there."

"Had houses. Ours is long gone. You know that. And, yeah, I probably met them, but..." He trailed off, lost in thought, and I wished I could crawl into his brain and find out what was going on up there.

I was just about to say, "Earth to Mac," when he leaned up on his elbow and stared down at me, his eyes more serious than I thought they needed to be. "Did I ever tell you about all that time I spent on Tiger when I was a boy? We swam and built bonfires and told lies, and I don't know what all. The Gullahs treated us like we were their own kids. We literally grew up together, some of us."

I touched his lips. "So maybe you still have friends out there."

Mac fell back into his pillow. "Nah. Time changes things, Maddy. I doubt a single soul would remember me."

"But you *must* know Baby's people."

"Not really. Our house was on the northern tip and theirs is closer to the southern end. I still don't know how their house survived Hugo and ours didn't."

"Why didn't y'all rebuild?"

"Too hard. Too much hassle. Too much money. And besides, if memory serves me, I was a handsome resident chasing after a beautiful young Pink Lady right about then."

I lifted his hand to my lips and kissed his fingers. "You know," I said, "you might be surprised. I mean about anybody out there remembering you."

"I don't think so, Maddy. That was another time. People change, move on. But back to my original point." He pulled me close. "Won't you girls at least consider staying in Charleston?"

"Why on earth, honey, do you mind us going to Tiger Island so much?"

"Maybe, just maybe," he said, cupping my face in his giant hands, "it's because I love my wife. And I

don't want to be away from her for two whole weeks.
Maybe I've gotten spoiled these years, having you all
to myself."

I traced his lips with my finger and whispered,
"Just think how you'll feel after all those days spent
away from each other."

We kissed and one thing led to another as such
things are wont to do. When all was said and done, I
drifted to sleep, dreaming in fits and starts of a baby,
and even as I dreamed, even as I saw her crawling
across my kitchen floor, I knew it would never come
true.

*   *   *

Two months later, the three girls of August and Baby
Gaillard loaded up the SUV and Mac drove us out
of Charleston. Our destination? A rickety dock on
a nearly deserted stretch of coast located just past
the southernmost point of Cape Romain National
Wildlife Refuge. Baby texted and prattled all the
while. No one, not even Rachel, could have accused
her of being unable to talk and use her thumbs at the
same time.

"Y'all are all Teddy talks about," she said, tapping
her smartphone's keyboard with one hand and pulling
her blonde curls over one shoulder with the other. "He
says he wants me to be one of the girls of August

when I grow up. Ha!" Judging by the *whoosh* sound, she'd evidently just sent a text into the ether. "That Teddy, he sure is a funny guy."

"In the unlikely event that ever happens," Rachel said under her breath, glowering out the window.

Baby guffawed. I'd give her that: She had a big-girl laugh and she wasn't afraid to let it rip. "When I grow up! I said to him, 'Why, sweetheart, I AM grown up. Lookee here. I have the boobs to prove it!'"

"How does he stand one minute—" Rachel started, snapping her gaze from the window and aiming it at Baby.

This was going far worse than I had imagined.

"Now, Rachel," Barbara interrupted, clipping short what was surely going to be a cut-to-the-bone quip, "you know as well as I do how gullible grown men can be in the presence of a pretty young woman." Barbara adjusted her big moon-shaped sunglasses and shot Baby a venom-dripping fake smile.

I was actually taken aback by Barbara's appearance. She had lost a good ten pounds since I'd seen her in June, had a new hairstyle with lovely platinum highlights, and had pretty much replaced her school-marm charm with sexy cougar sass. "Men don't think straight when a pretty young thing walks into a room. They drool in places we don't even know about."

"Thanks so much for the vote of confidence," Mac said, adjusting the rearview mirror, probably to get a better look at the girls.

"How old are you, anyway?" Rachel asked, pulling a sterling flask from her boho bag.

Baby tugged on a halter top that barely contained her boobs—she really did have a nice rack, as Mac so demurely put it—and said, sweet as the first dew, "I am twenty-two years old, which is, I believe, close to y'all's ages when you first became the girls of August. I have a degree in pharmacology from the University of Kentucky—go, Wildcats! But I don't work, not now, anyway, because Teddy says we have all the money we need. I can recite all of the US presidents in the order they served in under one minute. And I am fluent in Arabic."

"No you aren't," Rachel spit.

Mac started laughing that low, rumbling growl that takes over when he's truly tickled.

"Yes, I am," Baby said. And then, in a breathtaking show of not getting it, rather than speaking Arabic, she proceeded to—very rapidly—spout off the entire presidential roll call. I didn't know if it was a parlor act or not, given that I couldn't keep up with her, nor did I know if Fillmore came before or after Pierce. And how did Grover Cleveland get in there twice but not consecutively? I gazed at her pretty pink lips, which were moving at the speed of light, and the smattering of freckles that moved in tandem with her words, and I thought for a moment that I had underestimated the child. I looked at Rachel, who was taking a pull from her flask, and then at Barbara, who watched Baby with all the disdain one casts at a bad lounge act, and decided that no, if anything, I had given Baby Gaillard too much credit.

"Ta-daa!!!" Baby said brilliantly after "Obama" rolled off her tongue. And then she started texting again. *Tap, tap, tap, tap, tap!*

"Give me some of that," Barbara said, taking the flask from Rachel. In as ladylike a manner as possible, she took a sip, dabbed the corner of her mouth with her pinky, and said, "These kids' thumbs are going to look like thighs one day."

"Who are you writing?" Rachel asked.

"Texting," Baby corrected her without looking up. "I'm texting."

"OK, who are you *texting*?" Rachel let the word drop off her tongue as if it were dung.

"Friends. Teddy. Mostly friends though because Teddy's too busy." She gazed into the screen, her eyes scanning her latest message, and started laughing.

Barbara said, "That's all my kids do. They don't even e-mail anymore."

"They text during physical exams," Mac said. "Joe told me a young woman was in for a pap smear last week and she texted her way through the whole damn thing."

The image of a woman in stirrups texting away as the doctor inserted a speculum hit me as hysterically funny. Soon my giggles bloomed into all-out guffaws. Barbara joined in, tears streaming.

But not Rachel, who wasn't just annoyed at Baby—she was clearly hostile—and not Baby, who appeared to be fascinated with her latest message, her bright eyes scanning the tiny screen. While Barbara and I held our sides and howled, Baby began clicking away again, the fake keyboard sound a counterpoint to our laughter.

"Oh, for God's sake!" Rachel snapped, and before we realized what was happening, Rachel rolled down her window, snatched Baby's phone, and hurled it out.

Baby looked up, her green eyes wide, her mouth caught in a shocked, open-jawed silence. Barbara and I haltingly quit laughing and Mac scrunched down deeper in his seat as if he wanted to be anywhere on the planet except here, in this car, with an angry woman and a hurt child, ferrying us to an almost un-inhabited island.

"Jesus, Rachel!" Barbara muttered, staring out the window and then taking another long pull on the flask.

This was not like Rachel. She might be a no-

nonsense kind of gal, but tossing a phone out of a moving car was out of bounds even for her. I shot her a what-do-you-think-you're-doing glance but she kept her gaze averted.

"There's no cell service out there anyway," she said, glaring into the distance.

We were traveling down a two-lane blacktop that was bordered by marsh on both sides. There was no way the phone could be retrieved, but Mac, who is as good-hearted as the day is long, started to slow down, and he caught my eye in the rearview.

I shook my head no. "It's all marsh grass and gators," I said.

Mac let out a heavy sigh and Rachel grabbed her flask away from Barbara. The sweet scent of bourbon mixed with the bracing salt air and the stink of decaying vegetation. *It's all that dead stuff that makes the marsh muck so rich*, I thought ruefully, regretting I had ever agreed to this little outing. My stomach lurched and I was afraid I was going to be sick.

"Baby, do you want me to call Teddy when I get home? Tell him to buy you another phone so that you've got one waiting for you when you get there?" Mac, the peacemaker.

Baby, grim-lipped, nodded yes, but she did not speak.

Rachel rolled her eyes. Barbara refreshed her lipstick. I pressed my hands against my belly and took a few deep breaths.

And that's how we traveled the rest of the way, to what could be described as the end of the earth, in silence, fuming, Baby's bottom lip trembling as she fought back tears, sea light and birdsong all around.

*   *   *

Fossey Pearson was as barnacled as his boat, an old wooden-hulled retired shrimp trawler named *Miss Lucky Eyes*. The boat's name struck me as particularly hilarious given the fact that grizzled Fossey Pearson had only one eye and precious few more teeth.

"Got here just in time," he said, popping out of the wheelhouse and keeping his singular gaze aimed at Baby. He stepped onto the pier and put out his hand. "Good afternoon, Ms. Gaillard. I mean Patterson. Nice to see you again. Tide's just about to turn." He nodded in the direction of a barrier island rising like an emerald out of the blue Atlantic. "*Miss Lucky Eyes* can't get over to Tiger in a full-moon low tide. So, ladies"—his cigar bobbed from one side of his mouth to the other—"fire your engines. There's no time to waste." Then he aimed his good eye at Mac. "You coming too?"

"No sir. Just the ladies." Mac had donned a pair of

aviator sunglasses, pulled his ball cap seriously low, and slipped on his windbreaker even though it was hot as blazes. If I hadn't known better, I would have thought he was trying not to be recognized.

Fossey stayed in motion, unburdening Baby of her small overnight case. "Everything on board! Right now!"

Mac, who was carrying four duffel bags because he truly is a Southern gentleman, whispered in my ear, "It's not too late."

But Fossey—his gruffness, his decayed charm—had rekindled my interest in Tiger Island and our time together. Rachel would calm down. I would make sure of it. "Not on your life," I whispered back.

He nodded, sensing my resolve. "Everybody got everything?" Mac asked, dumping the duffel bags aboard.

"Coolers. We need the coolers. And Baby, let's go help Mac with the grocery bags," I said.

She looked as though she might go into a teenage sulk but evidently thought better of it. "Sure," she said breezily, walking toward the SUV, adjusting her short shorts. "Gawd, I can't wait to get out of these clothes and into the water."

"Clothes? That's what she calls that getup?" Rachel hissed, wiping sweat off her upper lip and then hoisting a bag into Fossey's sunburned, scarred arms.

"Just wait, we'll all be half naked with her before you know it. And it's not just her. Nobody her age wears clothes anymore," Barbara said, thrusting a second bag at Fossey, who appeared to be winded: His cigar was drooping.

"Y'all plan on staying the whole doggone month?" he grumbled.

"A prepared gal is a happy gal," Barbara said brightly.

"Is that so?" Fossey said, taking in her sweet, angular features, her jaunty ponytail. "Well don't that beat all."

"Mr. Pearson, I do believe you're flirting," Rachel said, and for a moment her tense visage gave way, revealing the old, playful Rachel of a couple of hours ago.

"A man might age," he said, hoisting up his beltless pants, "but an old salt like me"—he winked that faded blue eye—"never gives up."

Barbara beamed, her fresh red lipstick glowing in the high-noon sun.

"He comes from an old, old family who have been in these parts forever," Baby whispered as we made our way down the dock. "His great-grandmamma was a Cherokee princess and his great-granddaddy was a Gullah king. A very important man, his great-granddaddy."

"Really?" I asked, sizing up the bent, sunburned

old man who was gallantly taking Barbara by the hand and helping her aboard. "Well, whatever he is," I said, adjusting my bag of kippers and saltines, peanut butter and bread, "he's our only way on and off the island, so I hope his royal heritage keeps him on the straight and narrow."

"Hurry up, ladies," he called to Baby and me as Mac lifted the final cooler onto the deck. "The tide waits for no man," he bellowed, his arms outstretched as if he were Poseidon himself.

The sun was high overhead, bleaching the world of color, and I again felt sick to my stomach.

Mac pressed the back of his hand to my cheek. "Are you OK?"

I touched his hand and an odd urge to weep welled up inside me. I suddenly had no idea how I could spend two weeks without him. I flung my arms around his neck. "I love you so much, Mac."

"I love you too, sweet pea," he said. He held me by the shoulders and looked at me sternly. "You need anything, I mean anything, head over to the village. Ask for Mama Bonaparte. I don't know if she's still alive, but if so..." He trailed off. "It doesn't matter. The Gullahs will help out if you girls get in a jam."

He kissed me good-bye and whispered he would miss me. I heard the diesel engine blaze to life and one of the girls—I think it was Barbara—said, "Will you look at those lovebirds!"

Before I succumbed to a full-out faint thanks to the heat and the stickiness of the salt air, I pulled away. Mac helped me aboard *Miss Lucky Eyes* and we all waved at him as if we were about to embark upon a transatlantic journey.

"*Bon voyage*," Baby hollered, jumping up and down.

Mac stood on the dock, hands on hips, watching our departure. As the boat headed east, toward Tiger Island and away from the mainland, I gripped the rail, fighting seasickness in the moderate chop. For a while I kept my gaze pinned to the dock as Mac appeared to grow smaller and smaller, but finally I shifted it to the whitecapped sea because I didn't wish to see him disappear altogether.

*   *   *

Over the throaty backbeat of the diesel engine, with Bull Island off to our north, Fossey Pearson yelled, "We're coming up on her, girls. Tiger Island! Named for the tiger sharks that once swarmed thick as thieves in these shallows. Guess my granddaddy took his fair share of the fuc—um…monsters. I've been known to take a few myself."

"They won't really hurt you," Baby said. "Not unless you go swimming with a bucket of chum."

Fossey Pearson started laughing, pointed at her as

if he were pulling a trigger. She smiled back at him and actually batted her eyes.

"What do you know about chum, Baby?" Rachel asked.

Baby didn't answer. She seemed slightly afraid, as if there were a trip wire in the air.

"Don't underestimate Baby Gaillard," Fossey Pearson said. "Her people have been out here almost as long as mine."

Before Rachel could come back with something suitably acidic, Baby yelled, "Look!" She pointed off the back of the boat. "They're surfing!"

I turned and was delighted to see a small pod of dolphin—seven to be exact—surfing the boat's wake. "How fabulous!"

"Doesn't that beat all," Rachel said, making her way to the rear. Barbara, Baby, and I quickly followed.

"Aren't they beautiful!" Barbara said.

"Stare at 'em long enough," Fossey Pearson said, "and an ol' salt might think they're mermaids." He throttled down and took a more southerly route. "Right over there, that's where we're heading."

A dock, more rickety than the last, snaggled its way into a protected bay. I turned a full circle, taking in my new surroundings. The mainland was long gone. There were only sea, sky, and the approaching island. We had certainly gotten what we'd always said was one of our criteria for these August getaways: isolation. Only this time it was absolute. We could not pile into a car and go buy groceries. We could not nip over to a liquor store. We could not call up our husbands or kids and check in. Fossey Pearson, with his one eye and his chugalug boat, was our sole means of conveyance to an island that offered nothing but whatever nature supplied.

Nevertheless, as Tiger Island came more clearly into focus, it reeled me in. Even from this distance, I was taken with its primeval beauty. White sands, clear water, coastal scrub leading into some sort of hardwood jungle hummock.

"How did your people ever find this place?" I asked Baby.

"My great-granddaddy made a lot of money in the stock market. Coca-Cola, mainly. And my granddaddy, he had a thing for the sea. So he, with Great-Granddaddy's help, built himself a house right in the middle of it." Baby gazed at the island that wavered in this bright sunlight, and I saw a calm come over her, as if Rachel's ditching her phone no longer mattered.

Fossey Pearson idled us up, slow and close, to the dock. He seemed fully in his element, as if the smell of diesel gas and the confusion created by too much sea salt and sunlight made him the happiest man on the planet.

"Now listen here," he said. "Baby knows this, but

I don't think she's ever been out here with just a bunch of *women*." His inflection suggested that we were little more than helpless, dumb creatures who were perpetually in need of masculine wisdom.

Rachel's eyes flashed. I saw her coil up, ready to pounce, but I waved her down.

"Choose your battles," I whispered.

Barbara seemed unfazed by Fossey Pearson's banter. Radiant, she took in our surroundings as though paradise truly were healing, as if nothing the one-eyed old salt could say—no matter how insulting or inappropriate—could pierce her armor.

"There ain't a damned thing out here," he said, gently nudging the boat against the dock. "I mean nothing. No place to get your hair done. No place to spend your husband's money."

"What about my money?" Rachel snapped.

Fossey Pearson laughed. "Nope. No place for that either."

Without being asked, Baby helped him tie up *Miss Lucky Eyes*, her butt cheeks bared to all who would look every time she bent over. The rest of us began gathering our provisions. I think we all felt the same need: Get off the boat; get on with this vacation. I had a sense that some of us were already thinking it couldn't end soon enough. And I hoped that as soon as we settled in, people's frayed nerves would ease.

"There's no phone. Ain't no cell service either,"

Fossey said, at which Baby had the gall, or perhaps courage, to giggle.

He helped us unload the coolers. "No computers. No TVs."

Fossey Pearson was enjoying this, I could tell by the righteous gait of his words.

"No coffee shops. No shopping malls. No place to get your nails painted. Hell, they ain't even a Laundromat out here."

The four of us stood on the dock, watching him unload the final bag full of all manner of items we had decided we simply couldn't live without, and quiet washed over us as it sank in that we were about to be totally on our own.

"One more thing," Fossey Pearson said, disappearing briefly into the wheelhouse and then emerging with a pail filled with what, at first glance, appeared to be fireworks.

"Here you go," he said, handing the pail to Barbara.

"What *are* these?" she asked.

"Railroad flares," he said, and he winked at her again before returning to the wheelhouse, and it occurred to me that it actually might be impossible for a one-eyed man to wink. Perhaps it was just an exaggerated, slow, and sultry blink.

The idling boat engine thumped more quickly. "If you need me this week," he shouted, pulling away from the dock, "light a flare on the beach. I'll be here shortly. After that, light a flare and hope for the best because I'll be in New York City."

New York City? "What do we do while you're gone?" I hollered, hating the sick rise in my stomach that recognized abandonment.

"Don't worry," he yelled. "There's bound to be somebody on the pier over to the shore. Or a boat out in the bay will spy the flare. You ladies ain't got nothing to worry about. And oh yeah, be careful of the storms. We've been having some nighttime doozies!"

Those were his last words, which we barely heard over the engine noise and the breeze that seemed intent on blowing his instructions to smithereens.

"Where do we go now?" Rachel asked, hoisting a duffel bag higher on her shoulder, squinting at the sun, her face drawn and piqued.

"This way," Baby said, and it dawned on me that a power shift had just occurred. This was *her* place. She knew its mysteries... what could kill us, what could delight us. Holy crap. Baby Gaillard was in charge.

She sauntered off the dock, overnight case in hand. When she hit the beach, she kicked off her flip-flops and turned toward us. "Just leave all that luggage be. We'll get it in as time allows. Not like there are any pirates out here." And she giggled.

"Sounds like a plan," Barbara muttered, "but I'll bring the wine."

We trundled south along the beach, in the heat and the mosquitoes, and just when all of us, save Baby, thought this was some sort of horrible joke, the house—the beautiful, beautiful white-shingled house—came into view.

Splendid, it was absolutely splendid, nestled among the trees, sea oats and beach rosemary and red rugosa roses spilling wildly all about.

"Wow!" Barbara breathed.

"Amen," Rachel said.

"It's beautiful," I whispered. The photo had not done the house justice and, for a moment, I was seized with envy, wishing this stately, if weatherworn, two-story Cape with its big ocean-facing windows and wide wraparound porches belonged to Mac and me.

This was a house, I decided, that echoed the ages: stories, laughter, tears, storms, ghosts. Its crowning achievement? A widow's walk complete with an antique lightning rod in which was embedded a cobalt globe that seemed to pulse in the late summer sun. If the Kennedys had been Southerners, this would have been their Hyannis Port, I thought.

For a moment we stood there, taking it all in. Us. The great house. The mighty and beautiful Atlantic. The wide beach and deep jungle. I looked behind me. Our footprints in the sand signaled, to any critter that cared, our presence.

"They look like the only footsteps this beach has seen for a hundred years," Barbara said.

"Oh, no," Baby trilled, hefting her case into her other hand. "Mine and Teddy's were all over this place just last week, getting the house set up for us." She spun around, surveying her queendom. Her confidence and cheekiness had returned in full bloom. "Seems like everywhere you look, you see Teddy, doesn't it? There. There. There. And there." She pointed to the trees and the footprints, the ocean and the house. The child behaved and sounded like a lovesick virgin. She patted her heart to drive home the point that Teddy was all hers.

For reasons that had to do with old love affairs and icy Kentucky roads and the fact that we'd never again share sweet, sweet moments with dear Melinda, I felt my Irish rise.

"No," I said, a tangled knot of stubbornness stealing my good manners. "Everywhere I look, I see Mac. Just Mac."

Barbara uncharacteristically snorted.

And Rachel? She actually saved the moment. "Come on, Baby Big Boobs. Show us our new digs."

CHAPTER

2

Perhaps it was the sun, the heat, the boat ride, all that sand, the stunning house—I don't know—but as the others ascended the steps that would take them into the cool sanctuary of Tiger's Eye, for that is how the neatly hand-painted sign in yellow and turquoise identified the place, I was suddenly caught up in a confluence of things past, memories from long ago that felt urgent and new.

I was a girl again, twentysomething, a newly minted Pink Lady. My memory was clear and un-flinching: I had volunteered to be a Pink Lady because I had decided that the last thing I should do as a single woman was go straight home from teaching third-graders, where I would, as recent history had taught me, sit in front of the TV with a pint of Chunky Monkey, adding poundage to my loneliness.

A coworker at Harrowbrook Elementary—Mrs. Blakely, a fifth-grade teacher and a woman known to look down her nose at just about anything that breathed—accused me in the teachers' lounge of volunteering for the sole purpose of meeting a doctor. "That's a poor way for a woman these days to behave," she had admonished me as she grabbed a Krispy Kreme glazed doughnut and nibbled at its tender edge.

I didn't respond to the old crow. I didn't have to because she was 100 percent wrong and I didn't feel like wasting a single brain cell on her. I was not trying to meet a man, much less one who would become a doctor. I'd been a serious student. Teaching was for me not just a job. For the few years I did it prior to opening my catering business, teaching was my avocation, a dream realized. Perhaps it had been my unconscious mind's way of telling me I wasn't going to have any kids of my own so I'd best bask in the glow of other people's children. And volunteering as a Pink Lady really was a favored alternative to spending nights alone. I felt that, in a very small way, I was doing something meaningful, helping out people who were facing some pretty steep battles.

I was nervous that first evening on the job. And my nerves manifested in my inability to do anything right. My first assigned task was that of greeter. What could go wrong? Just sit at the info desk, be pleasant, and hand out maps to folks in need of directions.

The first person to approach was an aged man who walked with a pronounced limp and whose face appeared paralyzed in a permanent wince. His left arm was crooked at a crazy angle, and I feared that he'd dislocated it. Perhaps he'd fallen off a ladder. Or maybe a chair had gone out from under him as he attempted to change a lightbulb or reach for something on a top shelf. I was all about answers and alarmed that a sick person who was obviously in need of treatment had come in through the wrong entrance. By the looks of him, he was lucky to be alive.

"Sir, let me help you," I said. "I'll get someone right away to wheel you over to emergency." I reached for the phone, but then saw an orderly loping down the hall. "Orderly!" I called, sounding more desperate than I meant to, but I knew no one's name.

The old man looked at the young man in white who was heading our way and then snapped his head toward me. "Orderly! Orderly! Listen, lady, I don't need no orderly, and I didn't walk in here to get insulted by the likes of you."

The orderly, whose name I would learn later was Larry, held up his hands and walked backward, laughing, as though entertained by the old man's grumpiness.

"Sir," I stammered. "I'm so sorry. I thought you were hurt."

"Why? Because I'm old? Let me tell you something. I KNOW where the hell I'm going. Yes, sir, I do." He began to limp down the hall that led to the bank of elevators. "Gonna see my son. Emergency room! I'll emergency room you, you stupid, know-nothing broad."

I couldn't help it. Horrified, humiliated, and hurt all in one great moment, I began to cry. Before I could reach for the tissues, a tall, sandy-haired resident, whose lopsided horn-rimmed glasses were downright charming, leaned across the desk and handed me a handkerchief.

"Don't let Mr. Phillips get to you," he said in a deep South Carolina drawl. "He's mean to everybody. It's what keeps him alive."

I accepted the handkerchief and dabbed my eyes. "I'm so sorry. I don't know why I'm crying."

"Probably because that guy is an asshole and ass-holes make all good people weep." He smiled, broad and unassuming. He pushed his glasses farther up the bridge of his nose, but they remained askew.

I laughed and the jangle of nerves at the base of my skull unknotted.

"So you're the new Pink Lady," he said.

"I didn't know news of my arrival had preceded me," I said, handing him back the handkerchief.

"Usually it's not big news. But we haven't had a new Pink Lady as pretty or as young as you since Vandy Medical Center opened its doors all those many years ago." He slipped the tearstained hanky into his lab coat's breast pocket, an ingratiating, gallant move in my book. And I couldn't help myself: I liked the dimples. He stifled a yawn—those legendary hours residents kept were no doubt taking a toll—but his blue eyes remained full of mischief. "I'm Mac McCauley. Resident. Family practice."

"Madison Nash," I said, fully aware that the good doctor was flirting. But I decided as his pager went off that with his earnest sweetness he was the sort of guy who made a better best friend than boyfriend. After all, boyfriends were supposed to be slightly dangerous, always on the brink of leaving. That way they kept you wanting more. It was messed up but true.

Dr. McCauley checked his pager. "Gotta run," he said. "Catch you later, Madison Nash."

I found myself rather breathless in his wake.

The rest of my three-hour shift, thankfully, proceeded without incident. I handed out maps and restocked the candy bowl and even managed to make my way to the cafeteria for a cup of coffee.

My timing was perfect. In the back, under an array of bright fluorescent lights, Mac sat with a pretty young woman also cloaked in a lab coat, probably a fellow resident, and I could see that they were engaged in animated conversation. I decided I had been wrong. He hadn't been flirting with me after all. He was just friendly. A guy like him wouldn't go for the likes of me anyway. He wanted someone who studied brain cells, not lesson plans. And then, I admonished myself, I was not here to find a man. I was here to help people.

"Remember that," I said under my breath as I headed for the coffee station.

*   *   *

It didn't take me long to figure out where I felt I belonged, where I felt I might be able to do some real good: the children's cancer ward. That's probably because, of all the people I dealt with at the Vandy Medical Center, the children who were facing death were the bravest souls I would ever come across.

The CCW is where I met Tiffany Hodges. It's also where I met Teddy Patterson.

Beautiful and terminally ill Tiffany Hodges. Twelve years old. Childhood leukemia. Acute lymphocytic leukemia, to be exact. Acute because it was moving fast, racing through her body like a winged demon, turning the lymphocytes in her bone marrow into death cells. She didn't stand a chance. But still, we—because humans are basically positive creatures who believe that fundamentally the world is a fair and just place—hoped for a cure, a remission, a full-blown saint-sanctioned miracle.

I met her in late spring, when the dogwoods were still in bloom. She was sitting by a window in the CCW's sun-room, a drawing pad on her lap, a tin of watercolors on the table beside her. She was bald and thin, her pale skin tinged with the lightest lavender possible. As I approached, she looked up and smiled. Radiant, her eyes sparkling, she said, "You're new here."

"Yes, I am."

She held up the drawing pad. "What do you think?"

She'd painted a giant yellow bird with bright-green eyes and purple lips stretched into a wide grin. The bird was perched atop the largest of the blooms in what appeared to be a field of giant sunflowers.

"You're quite an artist," I said, and I meant it.

She blushed. "I just do it for fun."

"Well, you're awfully good," I said, admiring the drawing. "Mind if I join you?"

She studied the painting for a moment, dabbing off a bit of brown paint from the center of the big flower. Then she looked at me, direct and unafraid. "Why?"

I shrugged. "I don't know."

"Is it because I have cancer and you feel sorry for me?"

"No. It's just...I've been on my feet all day and you're here all alone. Maybe you want some company."

"I'm pretty happy no matter what," she said. She closed the lid on her paints. "Most do-gooders stop coming here after a while. They can't cut it."

"Maybe I'm not a do-gooder. Maybe I'm just hanging out." I appreciated her directness even though it was unnerving.

"So, what's your name?" She gazed at her painting as though sizing it up.

I tapped my tag. "Maddy."

"It says, 'Madison.'"

"Well," I said, sitting in the chair opposite her, "my friends call me Maddy."

"So, Madison"—she ran her hand over the smooth surface of her head and then looked at me with an intensity usually reserved for cross-examinations— "what's your favorite color?"

"Depends."

"On what?"

"My mood."

"Hmmm...me too." She blew on the drawing, I suppose to dry the paint, and said, "Today my favorite color is yellow."

"Why's that?"

Even without hair, she was such a pretty little girl. And her face betrayed no pain, no fear.

She set her painting on the table and looked out the window, which perfectly framed a sprawling old oak tree. In its near branches, a female cardinal offered a seed of some sort to her male partner. "Because you can walk through it. Yellow doesn't end. It just goes on and on and on."

I didn't know what to say. I suddenly found that I was in way over my head with Tiffany Hodges. Was she seeing her own death? Was she quietly refusing it? Or was she simply talking about her favorite color?

"Would you like one of these?" I asked stupidly. I reached into my pocket and withdrew some hard candies. She chose two—butterscotch and cherry.

"Thanks," she said and then again turned away from me, staring out the window into a distance I could not determine. "If you don't mind, I'm just going to sit here for a spell."

"No. I don't mind at all. I'll catch up with you later," I said, standing.

Twilight shadows were beginning to gather. The light glowed warm and golden on her face, and she looked beatific, or at least at peace with whatever might or might not come next.

I turned, ready to sprint down the hall, feeling that I had somehow fallen short in my job as a Pink Lady, fearing that those damned tears were imminent. Wasn't I supposed to offer confident cheer and support? Why did I feel Tiffany was onto me, knew that I didn't have a clue about what she faced and, indeed, had already faced? How did she know that though I had worked hard to carve out a career for myself—however inglorious, given that many of my students' parents did not seem to value teachers, indeed, perceived us as the enemy—I didn't know squat about the human heart?

I made a hard left, my intent being to leave the ward at the speed of light. But instead I found myself frozen in place, stunned to be returning the gaze of a man who was, despite a small scar along the cleft of his chin, bone-chillingly handsome. He looked like the kind of man who knows that the world is truly his oyster, that it speaks to him more kindly than it speaks to others. In short, he looked dangerous, as if no woman would ever keep him. And as I stared at him—his dark, wavy hair was combed directly back with every strand in place—I realized that it wasn't his looks that I found so compelling. It was his confidence. A surety smoldered in his steady gaze, which was too sophisticated to betray his thoughts. How could he seem mysterious yet guileless at the same time? He was a wonder, this one. There I stood, in defiance of my own advice, smitten at first sight.

"So, she got to you, did she?" he asked, nodding his head in Tiffany's direction.

"You could say that," I stammered.

"She has a way about her...I don't know. It's like she unlocks your secrets and shakes them in your face, but without malice."

He looked at me with what I interpreted as frank earnestness, offered me his hand, and said, "I'm Teddy Patterson. I don't believe we've met before."

Oh yeah. This guy was way more dangerous than Mac McCauley. As I slid my palm into his—a seal sliding into water—I felt myself fall into something that resembled ladylike lust.

Teddy seemed to take in the totality of me—my intellect and passion, my mind and heart—with those aquamarine eyes, and my whole body, against my will, blushed. His hand was much larger than mine, and that fact alone made me feel wanted, less alone. I must not have possessed much self-esteem to let the size of the man's hand turn me into jelly. In retrospect, I believe I was experiencing nothing more than a small but persistent hormonal storm. However, no one could have convinced me of that as we stood gazing at each other in the antiseptic glow of the CCW.

For a time it was glorious. He worked long hours as a resident, and he was singularly focused on his soon-to-be career as a pediatric surgeon, a career that I felt dovetailed beautifully with my desire to have four children. But despite that clear-eyed commitment to our careers, we managed to spend plenty of time together. Coffee breaks at the hospital. Dinners when we both had evenings off. Long late-night walks along neon-lit city streets. Then there were the movies and random parties.

Within a month our pronouns had changed. *We* like piña coladas. *We* don't like to do anything before ten on Sundays. Yes, *we* will be happy to come to your Halloween party. Within two months we were a bona fide couple. Within four I couldn't help myself: I sometimes dreamed of baby names. *Claudia. Tobias.* At six months, when I thought about the future, for the first time in my life, I saw happiness. I saw a life built out of the desires of two people in love. I saw children and houses and holidays and all the family trappings wrapped in shades of yellow, for I believed in what Tiffany Hodges had said: *Yellow doesn't end. It just goes on and on and on.*

I met people—Rachel, Oliver, Hugh. Mac and I became dear friends, and I did recognize but didn't fret over the fact that I was perpetually delighted to see him. All of us hung out together, had dinner at each other's apartments, gossiped about mutual friends and enemies.

And then came the Christmas party held at the Hermitage Hotel, that grand old dame bejeweling downtown Nashville with its ornate columns and arches, its gleaming paneled rooms alight with chandeliers and sconces and candles and cut crystal vases.

We'd pretty much overtaken the hotel—a band called Rufus and the Sliders played top forty in the ballroom. When they tired of dancing, residents, doctors, wives, girlfriends drifted into the comfort of giant couches in the magnificent, skylighted lobby. Those who'd had enough of the music and wanted to talk quietly or intently drifted into the Oak Bar for martinis or sodas.

We were dressed to kill in silks and tweeds and stockings and all manner of finery that glittered. I wore a black ruched dress that fit me like water on steel. It was cut low in front, lower in back. I was taking a chance in this dress. It was a take-no-prisoners statement, but still decorous, only hinting at danger.

Teddy held me close as we danced to Lionel Richie's "Hello." We slowly swayed to and fro and when he sang sweet and low into my ear the lyrics "And I want to tell you so much, I love you," I thought I'd grown wings and flown to heaven.

The song ended and I didn't know how I was going to do it, but I was determined to make my way to the restroom and gather myself. I caught Rachel's eye. She slipped from Oliver's grip and, being a girlfriend with a sixth sense, rushed over and said, "Teddy, I'm borrowing your sweet gal for a moment. We've got to powder our noses, don'tcha know."

"Well, don't borrow her for too long," he said, kissing my cheek. "I might get lonely."

"Fat chance," Rachel shot back and she looked at him as if he wasn't fooling her or anyone else.

Her stance confused me, but in my state of momentary exultation, I ignored any possible chance to feel anything other than supremely happy.

I took her arm and she steered us over to Barbara, who had just planted a sloppy kiss on Hugh's big face.

"Girl time. Let's go," Rachel ordered, her voice deep and clipped.

Barbara, who was obviously tipsy and dressed in a skintight zebra-striped sheath (those were very bad fashion days), wiggled her fingers at Hugh. "I'll be right back, baby!"

She stood, wobbly in her bejeweled black stilettos. A crooked smile crept across Hugh's face and he slapped her on the ass.

"Dr. Fowler," she cooed, "behave yourself!"

The three of us linked arms, drifted out of the ballroom, and made our way through the lobby and finally into the ladies' room. I fanned my face with my hand. "Oh my God!"

"What, what's going on?" Rachel asked. "You're acting like you're fourteen." She opened her evening bag and withdrew a cigarette.

Barbara hung on to the counter and said, "Woooo. I think I've had too much bubbly."

"Listen!" I said, happiness coursing through me like a sparrow on the wing. "I think Teddy told me he loved me!"

Rachel took a drag and blew the smoke in a roiling stream, angling it so that it missed her eyes. "Really?"

Barbara squealed and then threw her arms around my shoulders. "Yay!"

Her reaction was unreliable at present, so I focused on Rachel's. "I think so."

"What do you mean, you think so? Either he did or he didn't."

"This is wonderful news," Barbara said, slurring every single word. She let go of me and stumbled backward but the wall caught her.

"He sang me the 'I love you' lyrics." I turned to the mirror, opened my bag, withdrew my compact, and dabbed the shine off my face, watching Rachel all the while. She seemed impressed.

"Hmm." She cocked her head and took another drag. "That beats all."

"What do you mean?" Even I noticed that my voice lowered a register as I asked the question.

Barbara wobbled over to the love seat in the corner. She kicked off one shoe. "Don't let me drink any more."

"Look, honey, don't get me wrong. It's just that Oliver said the other night that he was a little worried. That you looked so smitten and happy. And, well, he thinks Teddy isn't ready to commit. Something about guys being guys."

"What are you trying to say?" I knew he could go

out with just about anybody. But had I fooled myself into thinking he actually liked me, that I was somehow special?

Rachel shook her head as if freeing it of stupid thoughts. She pulled out a tube of gloss and painted her bottom lip. She paused and, holding the gloss aloft, said, "Obviously Oliver is wrong. Just look at you! And look at Teddy!" She leaned into the mirror and glossed her top lip. With the job done, she said, "I think you two were made for each other. And you know what I always say..."

"What's that?" I asked, choosing to believe in her upbeat assessment and block Oliver's words from my mind.

"Lyrics never lie." She stubbed out her cigarette in the sink and we started giggling.

Barbara kicked off her other shoe and curled up on the love seat. She yawned and then, within seconds, fell sweetly asleep.

"Goodness! I've never seen her this smashed before," I said, walking over to her. She was snoring, light and breathy, like a child. "What should we do?"

Rachel glanced over her shoulder. "Just let her sleep. We'll tell Hugh he needs to take her home. In fact, they ought to take a taxi. He's pretty smashed too."

Her words slid right off me. In truth, I had only one thing on my mind. I went back to the mirror, fluffed my hair, refreshed my lipstick, and hummed the aching, soft refrain, hearing the words in my mind. *Hello, is it me you're looking for?*

Rachel lacquered on more mascara. She looked as if she could have been Raquel Welch's not-quite-as-glamorous, shorter sister (in my imagination Raquel was eight feet tall). Rachel stared at herself in the mirror, a warrior queen ready to do battle. "Let's go get our men."

We headed out, greeting some women I only faintly knew as they made their way in and started laughing when they spied Sleeping Beauty. I didn't care. Nothing anybody could say or do would mar this perfect evening. We stepped into the glittering lobby. Rachel immediately spied Oliver by the stairs and whispered in my ear, "I'll see you later. And don't worry. I'll deal with Barbara and her sodden beau."

"Thanks, honey," I said, squeezing Rachel's hand before she drifted toward Oliver.

I headed back to the ballroom, assuming where I'd left Teddy was where I would find him. But as I picked my way through the happy crowd milling about in the lobby, I saw him. He stood, dashing in his charcoal three-piece suit, by the red love seat located directly under the domed skylight. He was in deep conversation with someone who was seated out of my range of vision. I started toward him, his possi-

ble admission of love propelling me forward, joy and
hope fueling my brief journey. And then I stopped,
suddenly aware of the hard floor beneath my feet,
because the person he was in conversation with offered him her hand, which he took, and when she
stood, my blood chilled. Blonde and stunning. Pale
and glimmering. Her strapless white gown flowed
like starlight. She was my opposite. She was Barbie-
doll, Daisy Buchanan beautiful. I was quirky, minor-
character attractive. She emitted not a single flare of
insecurity.

They walked toward the ballroom. Actually, she
glided. People with money could do that—glide
across surfaces the rest of us stumbled over. I froze,
paralyzed by the possibility that I'd been jilted in the
time it had taken to refresh my makeup. But then I
thought, *He can't do this to me. I won't let him*. That
was my joy talking. It didn't want to let go.

So I followed them. And I was right. Everything
was OK. She had a date. A new resident. I didn't even
know his name. Teddy handed her over. Everyone
was smiles and laughter. I walked over and lightly
tapped his arm.

"Oh, there you are! I've been looking everywhere
for you!" He kissed my cheek, and he smiled as if
he'd really meant those lyrics.

And my blood flowed again.

*   *   *

Mac had not been at the Christmas party. He pulled a double shift so more of his colleagues could go. And though he was in our circle of friends, he never stayed very long at our parties, nor did he have a steady girlfriend. Mac simply had friends. And everyone seemed to admire him. What was there not to admire? He was affable, almost always in a good mood, sweetly handsome, and generous to a fault.

Every time I arrived at the hospital for my shift, there would be two sugar cookies in my message box, wrapped in red cellophane and tied with a pink ribbon. For the longest time I thought the sweet gift was from Teddy. But one late afternoon, after I'd thanked him for them, he said indignantly, "Those are from Mac. Not me," as if he would never stoop so low as to engage in a gesture that suggested sap ran through his veins.

At any rate, the cookies always gave me the perfect excuse to go see Tiffany Hodges. One for her, one for me. We would talk about what she did not have: the future. She told me she wanted her first prom dress to be cornflower blue to match her eyes. She wanted to be both an artist and an archaeologist because artists created life and archaeologists studied it. She was iffy about children but definitely wanted a dog.

I loved Tiffany Hodges for many reasons, including the fact that she taught me about the power and grace you gain when you never feel sorry for yourself.

Two days after Christmas—I had seen Teddy only once since the Christmas party and that was for coffee in the cafeteria because his schedule, he said, had "exploded"—I took the morning shift simply because I could, given that I was on holiday break. There in my message box were the cookies. I grabbed them, thought I should seek out Mac and thank him, but perhaps I wasn't supposed to know the identity of my sweet tooth benefactor. After all, he'd never mentioned the cookies, so perhaps the proper thing to do was play along with the mystery.

As I pocketed them and headed up to the CCW, I thought, *Two birds with one stone*: I'd stop in and see Tiffany, who had spent Christmas at home, but was back with us because her white blood cell count had dipped, and perhaps I'd run into Teddy.

Tiffany sat in a wheelchair in her usual spot, by the window that looked out over the grand old oak. Her back was to me and as I approached, she turned around. I couldn't help myself. I caught my breath and then forced a smile. The child looked far gaunter than I was prepared for.

"Maddy!" she said. Her smile was as incandescent as ever but her startling blue eyes flashed something else, something that I would later decide had been brought about by her being in the company of pain and certainty for far too long. We all know we're going to die, but we spend most of our lives denying it. Death was with Tiffany always. It was in the mirror each time she dared look at her reflection. It was in the IV drip that sent pain meds and chemo into her failing veins. It was in every numbered breath she took.

She reached out to me and I started to unwrap the cookies so that I could place one in her waiting palm. "No," she said, "give me your hand."

And I did. She took mine in both of hers and studied it. She ran her fingers along the bony ridge of each of my knuckles. She traced my lifeline with the tip of her pinky. She moved on to my wrist, finding my pulse, and whispered, a note of wonder softening her voice, "Do you ever wonder what you will look like when you're an old lady?"

I gazed out the window. It was snowing. And the world was changing.

"Yes."

*   *   *

On New Year's Eve, after being off for two days, I again worked the morning shift. Rachel and Oliver were throwing a bash at Oliver's apartment. Teddy, in a hurried phone conversation, told me he would meet

me there because he would be working late. I was OK
with that. I had caught up with him the day Tiffany
studied my palm, over coffee and a shared slice of apple pie, but even then his pager had kept going off. So
I was looking forward to the party with an urgency
well reserved for lovesick teenagers.

I arrived at the hospital determinedly optimistic
about prospects for the new year and my life with
Teddy. I stamped my feet before entering the big double doors, the crunchy sound of ice being sloughed
off reminding me of a childhood Christmas we had
spent in Maine when I was six. I remembered the red
coat I wore and my mother's cigarette smoke hanging heavy in the cold, cold air. For some reason the
memory prompted a melancholy ache that threatened
to move from my spine into my heart, but I sloughed
that off too and bustled into the hospital with every
intention of spreading new-year cheer wherever I
could.

First and foremost: Mac's cookies. Yes, they were
there where they always were: in my message box
along with a couple of belated Christmas cards from
other Pink Ladies whom I barely knew. I pocketed the
cookies and made a beeline to the CCW. I wanted to
greet Tiffany bright and early. I pushed away thoughts
of what it must be like to greet a new year knowing
you're going to die.

I exited the elevator and rounded the corner, expecting her to be in her favored spot in the sunroom. No one was there so I headed to her room, thinking that perhaps they hadn't yet probed and prodded her that morning, allowing her to sleep later than usual. The canned laughter and exaggerated sound effects that were the telltale hallmarks of cartoons wafted from the rooms of other sick children. I knocked on Tiffany's door—it was slightly ajar—and walked on in.

But there was no Tiffany. Stripped: There were no sheets on the bed. There were no stuffed animals holding hearts or get-well-soon balloons. Gone were the photos of family and classmates. No flowers. No watercolors glowing with yellow blooms. I spun around: no chart.

I ran out the door and down the hall. Now the tears were streaming. I followed the corridor to its very end and took a left. Teddy would know. I would make him tell me everything. I bumped into a nurse but didn't bother with any excuse mes. Desperation had made me rude. Laughter drifted out of Teddy's office and curled its way toward me. His laughter sounded like champagne and crushed glass. Hers sounded like diamonds spilling onto a concrete floor. I burst through the door. I knew who it was before I even laid eyes on her: the beautiful Barbie-doll blonde from the Christmas party. Her hand rested on his and she seemed flushed with something wonderful: the emergence of fresh love.

"Why? Why didn't you tell me?" I hissed.

Teddy leaped from his chair. Her mouth puckered into a tiny, confused, bright-red bud.

"Oh, Maddy, I didn't want you to find out like this. It's just...Cornelia and I met and well, these things happen. And I haven't had a chance to talk to you. I've wanted us to sit down and—"

"Tiffany. I'm talking about Tiffany," I sputtered, too shattered to acknowledge anything he'd said.

Cornelia excused herself, saying, "Well, I see you two have a lot to discuss." She stood, and her beauty and her Chanel suit made me wilt. "I'll see you later." She wagged her fingers at Teddy and then, as she walked past, placed a sympathetic hand on my shoulder.

I flinched but didn't take my eyes off Teddy, who, it appeared, didn't handle confrontation very well.

Teddy stared at the floor. He sighed. And then, "She died last night."

"What time?"

He raked his fingers through his dark hair. "Around eight thirty. Her body just couldn't take any more. We couldn't get her WBC up and..." He trailed off.

"Why...didn't...you...call...me?"

And then I knew. He hadn't been working at all. He had lied to me. It was as fresh as her scent on his lips. He had been out with *her*.

I was about to lose control. I was about to cry

in that loud, gulping, totally ungracious manner that prompts people to laugh at you. Or flee. And I didn't want to pummel Teddy with his lie. I was above that.

So I ran out of his office and fled to the closest safe space: the closet around the corner and four doors down. I slumped to the floor and wept bitter tears. I was racked with grief, heartbroken, embarrassed, pathetic.

Why had I let myself fall for the likes of Teddy Patterson? My first instincts had been right *and* wrong. Like Mac, he didn't want a girl who spent her Saturday mornings creating lesson plans. No sirree, Bob! Not Teddy! He wanted one who had breakfast with her banker.

I reached for a towel in a stack to my left and buried my face in it. As I wept, I heard the door open. *Please, God, no, no, no!* I had nowhere to run. I couldn't fit under the bookcase because it was flush with the floor. There weren't enough towels to hide behind. I didn't have enough time to scurry behind the trash bin or that pile of fresh sheets. The dust mop offered no help at all. I was screwed. I'd just been caught crying like a schoolgirl over spilled milk. I decided my best bet was to keep my face covered with the crying rag. Whoever it was would never be able to identify me. Plausible deniability: That was the ticket. Whoever it was would decide they'd stumbled across a crazy person and simply go away.

But that, of course, is not what happened. The stranger knelt beside me, pushed my hair out of my face, and whispered, "Hey. Come on. Don't cry."

"I'm sorry," I said, my voice muffled by the towel.

"You could find somebody so much better to cry over, you know."

"Who?" I whispered.

He took the towel away from my face and gazed at me, his glasses still lopsided.

"Me. I know I can't help you about losing Tiffany," Mac McCauley said, dabbing my face, wiping away my tears, "but that other guy? Why, he ain't nothing more than a twenty-four-hour flu."

And that's how it all began, on the floor of the broom closet. Where once I had seen Teddy everywhere—his fingerprints dappled all over my future—I began slowly, day by day, moment by moment, to see Mac.

And even though eventually the deep ache in my empty womb would grow fierce, it would never mitigate my love for Mac. We were right together. No doubt about it.

Teddy and I were simply a bad fit, like hair spray and fire. As for platinum-plated Cornelia Colleton, I figured Teddy deserved every ounce of heartache she would ultimately mete out. Teddy and Melinda, however, they had been right together. She eased him, filled up the unnamable longing that stalked him. And then, she was gone and there was Baby. God knew that man needed to grow up way more than he needed a trophy wife more than twenty years his junior.

At the thought of Baby, memories of my soft beginning with Mac tumbled away, washed by the sound of the surf unfurling on Tiger Island's white sand. And in that bright sunlight my eyes watered. Or were they tears born of bittersweet remembrance?

I climbed the porch stairs and, in my imagination, I saw not only my footprints on the sand-covered wooden planks, but my husband's. They were right there beside mine, step for step, heartbeat for heartbeat.

CHAPTER

3

The house was as fabulous inside as it was outside. The living room was big and breezy with a comfortable mix of white wicker and natural rattan furniture, all covered in vintage tropical-print bark cloth—yellow with big red hibiscus flowers and opulent green leaves. Drapes in the same fabric were pushed wide open, revealing the bank of nearly floor-to-ceiling Atlantic-facing windows. The house was easy—wide-plank pine floors, railroad-board walls painted bright white, at least three fireplaces (I definitely would have to go exploring), black-and-white family photos, and wedding photos of Baby and Teddy (she wore a skintight lace minidress and a veil that touched her bare shoulders). Gullah sweetgrass baskets were tossed here and there and everywhere, and seashells and sea glass sparkled on pine sills.

"Look at this pecky cypress coffee table," I exclaimed. "Where on earth did you find it?"

"My grandfather made it," Baby said, pouring us each a cold glass of white wine. "It's made from cypress that grew on his place on the Santee River. He could make anything. That's him as a little boy with my great-grandparents." Baby nodded in the direction of the fireplace centered in the wall adjoining the kitchen.

We all drew near and studied the image. A smiling couple sat on a glider and a little boy sat on the porch floor in front of them with a fishing rod held like a scepter. The woman's blonde hair was blowing in the breeze and the man's arm was slung over her shoulder, his fingertips grazing her neck.

"What a great picture," Rachel said, moving in for a closer look.

"Your grandparents and daddy?" Barbara asked.

"No! Great-grandparents and granddaddy," Baby said emphatically. "This is my daddy." She pointed at a handsome man in an Army uniform. They had the same nose.

I looked more closely at the first photo. "Oh! And it's this house!" I swirled around, taking in the room.

"Yep. When they were all young and pretty," Baby said, almost wistfully.

"Oh, my...you sure do favor your great-grandmother. She was stunning."

Baby, uncharacteristically, didn't respond. I glanced over in time to see her blush.

"Is this your mother?" Barbara asked, picking up a fading color snapshot of a woman holding up a glistening tarpon, the Atlantic in the background.

"That's her. Josephine." The timbre of her voice did not invite further exploration of that subject, so we moved on.

"You know what?" I said, my eyes flitting from one old treasure to the next.

"What?" Rachel walked over to a built-in bookcase and studied the titles.

"This place isn't a vacation home; it's a home home. Big difference." And though the exterior might have looked similar to that of the house owned by the first Mrs. Teddy Patterson, this was definitely not Cornelia Colleton's stuffy sterling-lace-and-porcelain house. A girl could get her groove on here.

"I'm glad you like it," Baby said. "I really am."

She was proud of this place, that was easy to see, and I began to understand why she and Teddy had been so insistent that we come out here.

"Well, Baby, what are you waiting for? We need the grand tour," Barbara said, and then she downed her wine and held out her glass for more.

We wandered from room to room, throwing open cabinet and closet doors without asking. Baby kept up a continual monologue about who had done what where, but mostly we didn't listen. We just oohed and ahhed and said, "Look at this!" to our hearts' content.

The kitchen was similar to a farmhouse kitchen, complete with a pantry, a butcher's block, a fireplace, a breakfast nook, a supper table, and an amazing AGA range. I admit, stone-cold envy took hold of me regarding that range, and I decided that when I got home, Mac and I would have a discussion about a remodel.

An enclosed sunroom with a sleeping couch and game table faced north, with a beautiful view of the dunes and beyond them, the ocean. Off the living room was a paneled library with three oversize cushy chairs. I could imagine Teddy lolling about in there, smoking cigars, drinking scotch, and reading his beloved historical novels.

"You haven't seen the best yet," Baby said, beaming, leading us upstairs, taking the steps two at a time.

"Good grief," Rachel grumbled, gripping the rail.

Barbara merrily shrugged her shoulders. "The privilege of youth," she whispered.

We crowded together on the landing, breathing heavily thanks to our attempt to keep up with Baby, and promptly fell into collective awe. "Jesus, Baby," Rachel said, while both Barbara and I, in unison, murmured, "Wow."

The landing was about a ten-by-ten area—virtually

its own room—and on the north side, to the right of the stairs, loomed a picture window complete with a cushioned seat. A person could curl up, read a book, nap, or just gaze out at the water and dream.

"You can see forever!" Barbara pressed her face against the window. "Amazing."

"My mama told me that Granddaddy brought a rocking chair up here and that's where we sat for hours. Mama rocking me to sleep, telling me stories, singing me lullabies. When Teddy and I have kids, I'm going to do that too."

"That's nice," I said, and I meant it, although her words—because they unintentionally opened up that nettle-filled crevice in my soul—made me wistful for what I didn't have.

"Let me show you your rooms," Baby said, heading down the hall that led from the landing. "We're all staying in the ocean-side rooms," she said breezily, "but if any of you want to move to the bay side, just let me know."

Tiger's Eye had six bedrooms, three with private baths and two with fireplaces. They all had four-poster beds and chifforobes. Chenille was everywhere.

"This is unbelievable," Rachel said, poking her head into first one room and then another.

"*Très magnifique!*" Barbara said, her college French slipping off her tongue.

"I thought you guys could take these three. They're side by side. The first two have their own baths. The last one...its bath is just across the hall. And I thought I'd sleep in the porch room—that's what we call it—because we made that part of the porch a bedroom after my little brother was born. I like that it's on the southeast corner. I dunno why."

"I've got dibs on this one!" Barbara said, walking into the first bedroom.

"Which one has the bathroom across the hall?" Rachel asked.

"Third one down. And it has a key if you want to keep everyone else out of it."

"All right. That's mine."

"Are you sure?" I asked. "I don't mind walking a few feet."

"I prefer it," Rachel said. And that was that. There was no talking Rachel out of something once she had made up her mind.

We spent the rest of the afternoon taking wine breaks and slowly getting our stuff up to the house and situating our rooms, which were lovely in every way, including their private exits onto the second-floor wraparound porch. Baby was helpful as could be, lugging our stuff and offering advice and saying things like "Lookee there! It's a dolphin!" and "That sure is a handsome osprey!" and "Hmmm, looks like that ol' coon got the turtle eggs. Blast his soul!"

Barbara was patient with Baby's constant chatter; she was a seventh-grade teacher, after all. But Rachel of Little Tolerance was having a tough time and would walk several feet ahead of us as we trundled from the dock to the house with our provisions.

When we were finally done, we sat in lounge chairs on the second-floor porch, wine in hand, enjoying the sea breeze that felt both cool and salty on our skin, and Barbara said, "I am pooped!"

"We oughta go swimming," Baby said, gazing out at the water, picking at a zit on her chin.

"I'm sitting right here. I am too exhausted to move a muscle," Rachel said, and then she yawned as if to prove her point.

"Why don't I fix us some sandwiches and we can eat them up here and then just fall into bed," I said.

"Can I help?" Baby asked, jumping up, her halter going askew so we all saw way more of her left boob than we had a right to.

I knew she was trying to be nice, helpful even. And sharing this house with us was wonderfully generous. But I just could not bring myself to take her up on her offer. I suppose that by then, I'd had enough of her prattle too.

"I'll tell you what," I said. "Why don't you go take a dip, these two can relax, and I'll fix us something to eat. I'll call you when dinner is ready."

"Great!" she said, throwing her arms around me.

Rachel mouthed the word *flake* and Barbara waved her hands in a move-her-along gesture.

Then Baby literally ran into the house, down the stairs, and onto the beach, where—to our profound surprise and dismay—she looked first left, then right, disrobed, and plunged buck naked into the ocean.

"Jesus H. Christ," Rachel said. "She thinks she's a freaking sea nymph."

"Two weeks? Two entire weeks?" Barbara reached for the wine.

"What did you say back in Charleston, Barbara? About killing her?" Any guilt over being mean about Baby was erased by my astonishment at her stark nakedness.

Rachel stood and rested her hands on the rail, not taking her eyes off Baby, who was doing the backstroke, boobs up. "Well, ladies, we might not have any choice."

*   *   *

I threw together a light dinner in that truly wonderful kitchen. There was something about this place, something to do with the generational comings and goings of a happy family, that made me feel at home. As I ran my hand along the stovetop's shining surface, I thought, *Maybe Mac and I should have adopted.* I imagined myself in my kitchen with a little towheaded girl, sprinkling sugar over star-shaped cookies. I closed my eyes and pushed away the image. We both had decided that maybe fate or God or the universe or whatever might be out there had deemed that it should just be the two of us. And that was how it was going to be.

"Spilled milk," I murmured. "No use fretting."

I flung open the fridge door and began gathering what I needed. I'd made the cold cucumber soup ahead of time, knowing that on our first night we'd be bushed. I found my fresh dill and sweet onions—garnish for the soup—in the crisper and set them on the counter. The bacon, lettuce, tomato, and Havarti on toast would be done in a flash.

As I went about the business of prepping these simple ingredients, a calm quiet took hold. Cooking always does that for me, unless the pressure is on because I am catering an affair such as, say, a large corporate party. But here, in this good kitchen, fixing food for my friends, I was at ease.

I reached for the knife that I would use to dice the onions.

"It's going to be a good August gathering, Melinda," I whispered. I peeled away an onion's skin.

"But we sure do miss you."

*   *   *

I made Barbara go down and get Baby. Rachel and I watched from the front porch. It appeared from the gesturing and Barbara's stunned expression that Barbara had to convince Baby to put her clothes back on. Barbara held open a beach towel, kept her head turned north, and did not watch as Baby spun herself into the towel.

"It's going to be a long two weeks," Rachel said.

"No. We're just going to have to ignore her when we can't take any more."

"Damn Teddy Patterson straight to hell."

"Let's eat upstairs, like I said. From there, we can throw her off the porch."

Rachel and I ferried the soup, which I'd put in a big Blue Willow tureen, and the sandwiches, which I'd tucked into a picnic basket I'd discovered in the pantry. As Barbara and Baby hit the door, I called over my shoulder, "Y'all bring the wine and napkins."

Baby was fussing. Something about having sand up her boopie because she'd had to put her shorts on.

I heard Barbara gently tell her, "Well go wash the poor thing out."

"Oh my God," I said and started laughing.

Rachel sighed and set her lips in a thin, grim line.

As I unpacked the basket, Baby wiggle-walked out onto the porch, set down a chilled bottle of sauvignon blanc, and said, "Ouch, ouch, ouch," before fleeing into her room.

"Drama queen," Barbara said as the screen door bounced on its hinges.

We gathered around the table we'd pulled over from the other side of the porch and heard the shower go on.

"Scrub that thang, girlie, scrub it!" Rachel said.

"What was going on out there?" I asked Barbara.

She poured herself a glass of wine and said, "She said it's a tradition she and Teddy started. Their first night on the island, they always go skinny-dipping."

"Did you tell her that Teddy isn't here and we don't want to see her bare bottom?" Rachel asked, reaching for a toasted BLT and cheese.

"*La soupe est délicieuse. En vérité divine.*" Barbara smacked her lips and even though I didn't speak French, I caught her drift.

"Thank you, Babs. And you, I must say, are looking good. You've lost weight since last we saw you. And your hair is gorgeous."

"Yeah. You look hot. What's going on? You cheating on Hughy?"

"Far from it," she said. "But thank you. I feel younger with that fifteen pounds gone."

"Should we wait to eat until she's out here?" I asked.

"Does it look like I'm waiting?" Rachel said with her mouth full.

I glanced over at Barbara, thinking she'd be laughing, but instead she looked anxious, as if perhaps my commenting on her appearance had upset her somehow. "You OK, Babs?"

"Yeah, yeah. Of course," she said. "Should we talk about chore assignments now?"

"Hell no. That will wait until Miss Crabby Coochie gets out here," Rachel said.

I snapped open my napkin, determined that our first shared meal on the island would not be ruined by Crabby Coochie's presence or absence. As I slipped my spoon into the velvety soup, I asked, "How are the kids?"

"They're fine," both women answered in tandem.

"And Curry?" Rachel asked.

"She's great. Seems to be loving Cambridge."

"Hope she feels that way once school starts," Barbara said. "But she should be A-OK. Smart girl, that one."

"Yes, she is," I said. And then we all fell silent, and not because we didn't have anything to say, but because this wasn't right. The set number was four. And Baby didn't count. She wasn't a girl of August. She just wasn't.

After about thirty seconds of our staring out at the ocean, not eating, not drinking, Rachel finally said, "Oh, Christ. Let's just get this over with. I will never forgive Teddy for taking Melinda from us. Never. I am still angry and still waiting for him to fess up that he was responsible."

"It won't bring her back," Barbara said. "There's nothing he can say or do to make it right."

"But it's his fault."

"I don't know, y'all," I said. "I imagine Teddy feels worse than anybody about the accident. I mean, he really, really loved her."

"He really loved who?"

We all jerked our gazes away from the water. There stood Baby, hair wet and combed flat. She'd slipped into a turquoise cotton shift. Barefoot, without any makeup on and sweetly tanned, the child was a natural beauty. I had to give her that.

"Melinda," Rachel said. "Teddy really loved Melinda."

Baby's face quivered and turned scarlet, as if she might be on the precipice of tears. As I watched her, willing her not to break down, it dawned on me that being the third Mrs. Teddy Patterson was no walk in the park. The other wives, to varying degrees, were always in the room.

She pulled a chair over and Barbara made room for her on her side. Baby surveyed the soup and sandwiches. Her face brightened. "This looks great!" she said, spooning several ladlefuls of soup into her bowl. She dipped her sandwich into the soup and then said, her mouth full, "He still does."

"He still does what?" Rachel asked, her eyes narrowing, snakelike.

"Teddy still loves Melinda." Baby wiped her mouth with the back of her hand. Evidently money did not automatically come with manners. "And that's OK." She glugged her wine, set down the glass, and, with barely a pause, said, "He should love her. I wouldn't want to be with a man who fell out of love with his dead wife."

Barbara did not conceal her surprise. "Wow! That's a great attitude, Baby. I'm sure Teddy appreciates it."

Baby nodded, her normally animated face still and serious. And *serious* looked funny on her, like when a little child tries to explain to a parent a situation she finds grave and inexplicable.

"I told Teddy that I think of her like my sister. And I want to do right by her." Then Baby said, "But I don't know if I can."

I glanced at Rachel, who was not convinced. She opened her mouth, and I was sure a poison-tipped arrow was about to fly, so I jumped in.

"Baby, Melinda was a very fine person. And we miss her something terrible. But that doesn't affect how we see you."

"Awwww! Thank you!" Baby's eyes brightened. "I just love you guys!" she said.

Rachel responded by making a clucking sound.

And that's pretty much how our first night on Tiger Island went. We ate good, simple food, drank lots of wine, divided the chores among us (I would play chef and Barbara would be my assistant, Baby would do the dishes, Rachel would take out the trash), and, as the nearly full moon rose up out of the water, we talked about silly things, dreams of little consequence. Baby wanted a diamond tennis bracelet for her twenty-third birthday, which was just three months away. "And a dog. I want a little dog that we get from the pound."

Rachel said that if she were rich, she'd give away every last penny, except she'd give a modest sum to each of her five kids. "Ollie could fend for himself," she said, and when she did, her voice broke. I looked at her sharply—she was not given to public displays of emotion—and I sensed there was some sort of trouble brewing, but on that night, under the glow of that big moon, I could not imagine what problems might be rattling Rachel.

Barbara said that if she could have anything in the world it would be that all her friends and relatives, both living and dead, would have a "big ol' soiree" and everybody would tell the truth about everything. "Talk about a reckoning!" she said, giggling, but the laughter did not reach her eyes, and I wondered if both she and Rachel had come on this trip with suitcases full of secrets.

"What about you?" Baby asked. "If you could have anything in the world, Madison, what would it be?"

I started to speak, but stopped. I knew if I uttered one word, I would burst into tears. That urge to cry, I told myself, was probably from the wine. I looked at Rachel first, then Barbara. They both knew what my Achilles' heel was: my barren womb.

Not having a clue, Baby said, smiling, "Well?"

"World peace," I blurted. "I'd want world peace."

Rachel guffawed.

Barbara said, "Let me find your tiara!"

"A queen is born!" Rachel crowed.

Then everyone but Baby started laughing. She looked at us, one at a time, as if we were off our rockers, her pert little face knotted into a scowl. "What's so funny?"

"World peace," Barbara said, wiping giggle-tears off her cheeks. "It's what bubbleheaded Miss America contestants always say."

"Shoot," Baby said, still clearly not getting it. "I always wanted to try out for Miss America but then I went and got married. You know, I can twirl a fire baton."

"You can?" I asked, happy to move the focus off of me.

She nodded yes. "If I can get some kerosene while we're here, I'll show you."

"Great!" Barbara said. "Wine and a floor show."

"Talent show," Rachel said. "Let's have a god-damned talent show while we're here."

"That would be wooooonderful!" Baby said, jumping up and spinning around before falling on her round behind. "Whoops."

"No more wine for you," Barbara said, pouring herself a refill.

This was nice. The sea breeze. The bright moon. The stars. The easy conversation. "Well, ladies," I said, lifting my glass while Baby scrambled to her feet and rubbed her bum, "welcome home!"

"Welcome home!"

"Welcome home!"

"Welcome home!"

We clinked glasses and Baby chugged from the bottle. And when the moon was nearly right above the house, causing the lightning rod with its cobalt ball to appear made out of quicksilver, we all hugged and then drifted to bed and no one said anything mean about Baby.

I do believe that each of us slept the whole night through without our real lives interrupting our dreams.

*   *   *

I will not deny that I am a superstitious woman. I avoid black cats when at all possible. I never walk under ladders. I believe that I must tell Mac I love him each time we finish a phone conversation or else something horrendous will happen. After all, you never know when a meteor might plummet from the heavens and strike your house. Or when squirrels will chew through the wiring in your attic, setting the whole house ablaze. Or when a nest of rattlers will take a liking to the dark space under your driver's seat...talk about an accident waiting to happen!

That being the case, and in order to ensure a rollicking good time with the girls of August, I had developed a full first-day ritual: Get out of bed before dawn and watch the sun levitate out of the pink waters. If I didn't, I feared all manner of mayhem could descend.

As my eyes adjusted to being open and as my brain slowly began to fire on all cylinders, I imagined the sun rising out of the Atlantic: the golds, the wild blues, the pink stain, the illumination of a dawning day. It promised to be stunning.

Not bothering to flip on a light, I slipped out of my pajamas and into my bathing suit in the dying darkness. I headed downstairs and into the kitchen in search of coffee. The heart pine floors were cool beneath my bare feet. Without the sounds of the wind and surf, Tiger's Eye would have been resolutely silent.

To my surprise, someone had already made coffee.

I opened the cabinet door and found an array of big mugs in bright colors. Baby was a bit of a challenge, but she obviously came from a happy and loving family.

Mug in hand, I pattered through the living room, eased open the front door, and encountered my second surprise of the morning. Barbara was sitting on the steps, staring at the water, holding her coffee cup in both hands. *It's OK*, I thought, cautioning myself. *This is not bad luck. This is good luck. Good, abundant luck.*

"Good morning, Barbara. Mind if I join you?"

"Maddy!" She patted the empty spot next to her. "Have a seat."

"You're up awfully early," I said, settling down beside her.

"Oh, well, you know...sleep, it's overrated."

She gazed into the distance and I felt a smidge guilty for having interrupted her reverie. She surely seemed lost in thought. And, if I were blatantly honest, the gathering cloud of crow's-feet around her pretty brown eyes deepened her beauty. "It's starting," she said.

I looked at the horizon. Indeed it was. A glimmering line of liquid silver broke the darkness at the edge of the ocean. "It's going to be a good one."

"Sure as hell is," and she reached for something by her left foot. "Bailey's?"

"My, my, Barbara! Of course." I held up my cup and she poured a healthy shot of sweet liqueur into my coffee and then did likewise with hers. This was a different Barbara. Up at the crack of dawn. Drinking at the crack of dawn. An assertive ease fueling her gestures. The Barbara I knew had always been a tad tentative. Rachel and I were the leaders of our happy band. Barbara had always followed us, a gentle acquiescence lighting her eyes. Now a fierce light burned, leaving no room for equivocation.

She stood and her hair unfurled from its loosely caught ponytail. I liked this new Barbara.

I followed her toward the ocean as the night slowly melted away.

*   *   *

After an hour or so spent walking the beach, watching the sun's ascent amid a purple-and-gold sky, agreeing that Teddy Patterson could tack the title "cradle robber" onto his personal résumé right after "gold digger," and sipping our spiked coffee, hunger pulled Barbara and me back to Tiger's Eye, where Baby and Rachel were still soundly asleep.

Barbara rinsed out our mugs and I studied the contents of the fridge. It was going on eight thirty and already I could feel our time slipping away. "You know what?" I said, looking over my shoulder. "This ain't no slumber party. I'll fry the eggs if you rouse those two out of bed."

Barbara scanned the kitchen, obviously deep in thought, as if a great idea were brewing. Then she grabbed a pan, a lid, and two big spoons. "We're *both* going to rouse them," she said, her eyes gleaming.

"Aha!" I said, perceiving her meaning.

We were a duet composed solely of cacophony. We marched through the living room and up the stairs, pounding on our makeshift instruments for all we were worth. The last time I'd behaved in such a fashion my bike still sported training wheels, and a training bra was nothing but a gleam in my un-made-up eyes.

We reached the landing and headed down the hall. Barbara paused in her banging only long enough to throw open Rachel's door and belt out a rewritten version of that old Tom Jones song. "Wake up, pussycat! Whoa-o-o-o-o-ah!"

Rachel groaned, rolled over, and pushed her burgundy-colored silk eye mask up on her forehead. Her blue eyes were heavy with sleep.

"What the..." She shaded her eyes and looked at us as though we were on fire.

"You cannot sleep all day, Ms. Grump-along," I said. "This is our first day in paradise, and we are going to have fun even if it kills us!"

"Big whoop," she grumbled. But she did throw

back the sheet, sit up, stretch, and yawn loud and long. "OK, guys," she said, removing the eye mask and tossing it on the white wicker side table, "you win." She looked bedraggled, as if sleep had done her no favors.

"Next up?" Barbara asked, her right eyebrow arched roguishly.

"Baby!" we both yelled, resuming our pot banging, our lack of rhythm no doubt aided by the Bailey's we'd ingested at sunrise. Giggling, we rushed out of the room as Rachel rifled through her sheets in search of something lost in the night.

Barbara paused for a moment and I nearly ran into her. Over the clanging, in a stage whisper, she said, "Ugh. I'm losing my enthusiasm." She nodded her head in the direction of Baby's room.

"No can do. She's one of us now."

Barbara narrowed her eyes. "Never!" She laughed like a madwoman and we took off again.

As we hustled down the hall, I thought that surely with all the commotion Baby would be awake. Barbara pounded on the door three times: "I'm gonna huff!" *Pound!* "And puff!" *Pound!* "And blooow your house down." *Pound!* Then she threw open the door. We clanked and hooted our way in. And then we stopped.

Baby *was* still asleep, laid out like a silk ribbon on top of the sheet. She wore a long nightshirt the same color as her hair. But the golden girl in slumber did not look like her giddy waking self. Rather, there was something about her—maybe it was the turn of her mouth or the one hand clenched into a fist—that made me sad. But her deep sleep piqued my concern.

"Is she dead?" I asked.

"Maybe."

"Wouldn't that just beat all?"

"Damn, she's got a good body," deep-voiced Rachel said from behind us.

Barbara stepped up to the bed and put her hand close to Baby's mouth. "Nope. Not dead. Just a typical teenager's sleep." And then she held the pot an inch from Baby's ear. *Wham!*

I feared that perhaps Baby had gone deaf overnight, because she simply sighed, opened her eyes, shot us a dazzling smile, and murmured, "Oh. Hi. Hello, girls." She looked around, appearing profoundly bemused, and asked, "What time is it?"

"Noon, you lazy butt," Rachel lied. "Now get out of bed and into your swimsuit. There are rays to catch and wine to drink."

"Y'all are the best," Baby cooed. She stood, stretched her arms over her head, arched her back, yawned, and seemed utterly unfazed by our two-gal kitchen pot band. Then, in a split second, a sudden glint of glee lighting her face, she whipped off her nightshirt—to our collective relief she wore a polka-dot bikini underneath it—and ran past us, shouting, "Last one in the water is a rotten egg!"

We heard the front door open and slam. The three of us looked at one another, astounded and, if I were honest, even a little bit envious. The child seemed to seize life in ways that had long escaped us.

"What the hell," Barbara said, taking the pot lid from me. "Fuck it. Let's go."

*   *   *

I was the rotten egg but only because as Barbara, Rachel, and I hurried out the door I suddenly became light-headed, as if all this sun and sand and glimmering water were exacting a strange toll on me. So I slowed down and made my way to the water's edge, steadying myself as the girls splashed in the waves. Baby bodysurfed and I called out, "You best watch out for stingrays, hitting the bottom like that."

She scudded, facedown, across the sand, the waves lapping over her. Then she jumped to her feet and spun around, ignoring my admonition.

I waded into the ocean, making my way over to Rachel and Barbara, who were both watching her. "What do you think?" I asked, realizing that we weren't even twenty-four hours in and already Baby had driven us crazy, made us love her, and then driven us crazy again.

"I think she's fucking nuts," Rachel said.

"She's exactly what Teddy deserves," Barbara said, splashing water. "That piece of tail is going to give him a heart attack."

For some reason I found this wildly amusing. I started laughing and the mirth took hold. I could not stop.

Rachel said, "No shit. Here lies Teddy Patterson, killed by his own wayward pecker." And then she and Rachel joined in my laughter. We were three howler monkeys being jostled by the waves.

"Hey! Hey!" Baby shouted above the surf. She stood at the water's edge, hands on hips, lips in a perfect pout. "What's so funny?"

"You would never understand," Rachel said, evidently not caring if she hurt Baby's feelings.

"It's an old joke," I said, my laughter slowly stuttering to a halt. "It's nothing."

Barbara whispered, "Yeah, don't worry your pretty little empty head over it." Then she kicked up her heels and floated on her back, bobbing amid the swells, her platinum-streaked hair spreading out like a corona. "Ahhhh. Glorious!"

Baby appeared to be thinking something over. And I could tell what it was. Fight? Or flight? But after a few moments of apparent contemplation, she chose neither. Instead she joined us. "I just love you guys!" she sang, repeating the previous night's mantra as she splashed into the water.

It was as though we were trapped in an episode of *The Twilight Zone*, all damned to repeat our roles: Rachel was about to blister Baby, Barbara was determined to ignore her, Baby was being obsequious, and I was the rescuer, playing Baby's protector.

"I want to thank you, Baby," I said as she approached. "This place is beautiful. Thanks for sharing it with us."

She nodded, smiling, but her eyes filmed over. "My parents are dead. My big sister lives in Paris, France. And my little brother is trying to break into the movies in Hollywood. So Teddy and I are the only two who ever come out here anymore. That's kinda sad, don't you think?"

"Yeah. Yeah. I do," I said, trying to stay upright in the waves, and wondering if she was toying with us. Arabic-speaking? Pharmacy degree? A sister in Paris and a brother in Hollywood? "Do your brother and sister have any kids?"

"Nope! Not my brother. He's too busy becoming a heartthrob. My sister has three kids but they're all Frenchies and look down their noses at me."

"Well then," Barbara said, still floating on her back, "it looks to me like you and Teddy have the whole damn place to yourselves. Not bad! By the way, *parlez-vous Français?*"

"*Leh, leh. Tatakellum Arabi.* I told you."

At least that's what it sounded like she said. And then she dove underwater, doing only God knows what. I scanned the swells. No sign of her.

"Don't worry about it," Rachel said.

"What did she just say?" Barbara asked. "It actually did sound like freaking Arabic."

"She's just fucking with us," Rachel said.

I started to count, panic rising one number at a time. I was on seventy-two when Baby shot out of the water as if from a cannon and gleefully shouted, "Wheeeeee!"

Relief surged through me, but so did resentment. I didn't like that I was being thrown into the role of babysitter.

Rachel swam over. "I'm going to strangle her," she said, wiping salt water out of her eyes. "Just you wait and see."

*   *   *

After our swim we were famished, so we threw together an easy brunch. Cheese omelets, grits, toast, strawberries dusted in sugar and blessed with a hint of Cointreau. And then, of course, there was that pitcher of Bloody Marys. Just what the doctor ordered.

Baby—who had been toasted a gorgeous golden brown by the morning sun—was preening, overly helpful, in her newfound role of I-know-where-everything-is-located.

Barbara cheerfully swilled booze and made sure our glasses never ran dry.

Rachel wasn't as grumpy as she had been earlier in the morning, but she seemed preoccupied, unable to shake off whatever mental baggage she'd dragged with her from her real life all the way to Tiger Island. She pulled a stool over to the butcher block where I sliced and diced, staring into space, her eyes blue with distance.

I stepped over to the stove, poured the whipped eggs into a sizzling pan, and promised myself that no matter the temporary cost, I would get to the bottom of whatever was eating the good Mrs. Oliver Greene.

"Remember that crazy old haunted house we rented down in Florida?" Barbara asked as she squeezed a lime wedge into her Bloody Mary.

"Oh, yeah…what was that place called?" I asked, grating a wedge of sharp cheddar.

"What place was that?" Baby asked.

"Started with an *s*…" Barbara snapped her fingers as if that would jog her memory.

Baby doused her Bloody Mary with several jabs of Tabasco, paused, and shouted, "Sanibel!"

"No, no, the other side of the state…Summer

House…Summer Hope. Summer Day…no, no, no wait, I've got it! Summer Haven!" Barbara crowed.

I sprinkled the cheese on the giant omelet that I planned to cut into fourths. "That's right. Old haunted house. Remember, Rachel?" I asked, trying to pull her out of her funk and into the present.

"How could I forget? I swear to God that ghost got in bed with me one night. The horny bastard tried to spoon me." Rachel reached across for a scrap of cheese and I slapped away her hand.

"Blame it on the ghost!" Barbara said.

"Ooooo, paranormal sex!" Baby trilled, arms akimbo.

Rachel glanced over at her and actually chuckled. "I almost wet the bed, it scared me so bad."

"You woke up the whole house. Remember? We were all scurrying around and bumping into each other. And then"—I reached for the spatula and shimmied it under the sun-yellow omelet—"Barbara, you grabbed that croquet mallet out of the corner by the front door!"

"And Melinda grabbed the basket of balls as if she was going to pummel the ghost, one ball at a time!"

We all started laughing except for Baby because, I knew, it was one of those you-had-to-be-there moments. Tears streamed down Barbara's face. As she wiped them off, she said, "Melinda and I were going to crack that ghost's head wide open."

Baby, despite what she'd said about Melinda the night prior, seemed unprepared for us to talk about her again. She stared down into her drink, her smooth brow furrowed, as though she were searching for a way out of the conversation.

I felt a pang of regret. This was Baby's house, yet Melinda had become the new ghost in the room.

But, proving she could occasionally behave like a grown-up, Baby recovered. She twirled her celery stick and licked the Bloody Mary off it as though it were a Popsicle. "And then what happened?"

"We all ran outside," Rachel said.

"In our jammies…and they didn't amount to much." I slid the omelet onto a sea-green serving plate.

"I don't even think I was wearing *that*. I remember grabbing a towel," Barbara said, topping off her drink.

"That's right!" The memory flooded back. "You held that mallet in one hand and kept the towel around you with the other. And Melinda…" I shook my head. "She said in that sweet, soft south Georgia drawl of hers, 'I swear to Jesus, I'll beam the fucker.'"

"Oh my God, that was a funny night!" Rachel said, and I thought her eyes teared up with mirth, or was it because life is so bittersweet? She looked at Baby and spoke directly to her, as if she were trying to teach her something. "We stayed out on the beach all night. We made Maddy go in for wine and chips."

"And she took the mallet with her."

"Yes, she did," Rachel said, still speaking to Baby. "And we fell asleep under the stars, that wonderful breeze blowing over us. And you know what?"

Baby's deep eyes were cat-wide. She bit down on the celery stick and chewed. "Nuh-uh. What?"

"None of us were afraid. We were the girls of August. Melinda. Maddy. Barbara. And me. We were like our own fabulous, light-up-the-sky constellation. And we knew that out there under the stars, with that big ocean singing to us, no one was going to break us up. Not man or beast or ghost. Nobody."

Baby didn't say a word. She just nodded. Like the rest of us, she probably didn't know if the words were a condemnation of God for having taken Melinda from us, or just something Rachel felt like getting off her chest.

"Well," I said, wiping my hands on a dish towel and lifting my glass, "here's to Melinda. Gone but not forgotten. Always a part of us. Forever loved."

"Hear! Hear!" Barbara said. "God, I miss her."

And we clinked our glasses and we drank. Baby too. And that's how it was supposed to be. Because if she truly wanted to be one of us, from the very get-go, she was going to have to deal with Melinda's ghost. It was one thing to say she felt as though they were sisters. It was entirely something else to live that sisterhood.

*   *   *

After brunch, Rachel and Barbara stacked the plates in the dishwasher and Baby wiped down the counters. As the cook, I put up my feet and watched them work.

"You know, I think that house on Dauphin Island was one of the best we ever stayed in," I said.

"You mean that old hippie joint?" Rachel looked over her shoulder at me.

"Yep."

"And why is that?" asked Barbara.

"Because nothing in it made sense. It was as if somebody would get stoned and say, 'Hey, there's a great place for a window,' and then they'd cut a hole in the wall with a hacksaw."

"How does that make it a nice place?" asked Baby, who then proceeded to suck something off her thumb.

I shrugged. "I don't know. It was original. The place was relaxing, no pretense."

"Don't forget the weed," Rachel said.

"Ooooo, the weed!" Barbara spun around, her eyes merry. "Mel found a bag of it under the deck. Remember? Somebody must have dropped it."

"Mel got stoned and went up on the widow's walk, ripped off her shirt, and shouted, 'I am queen of the world!' I thought that old man next door was going to have a coronary," I said.

"Actually, I think it extended his life." Rachel wiped her hands on a dish towel that was the same sea green as all the plates. "That girl had a body that could stop a train."

"She sure enough did," Barbara said.

Baby's face clouded over. She opened her mouth to say something but then seemed to reconsider.

"And that's the house where you, Rachel, pulled on your underpants and suddenly screamed bloody murder and we all ran in there and you were pulling them off, hollering, 'It's biting me! It's biting me!'" I could barely get out the words because I was laughing so hard.

"What was biting you?" Baby asked.

"A tiny scorpion, but you would have thought it was a ten-foot-tall rabid tarantula," said Barbara.

"I'm sorry," Rachel said, "but you let a scorpion sting your labia and see how loud you scream."

"I will never forget as long as I live you lying in that hammock with an ice pack on your coochie!" I got up from the table and hugged Rachel. Barbara joined in.

"You all are crazy, but I love you," Rachel said.

Baby the Outsider—in her own house, no less— stood there watching, and I felt certain she was waiting for one of us to wave her over, but the invitation never came. As Rachel planted a kiss first on my head and then on Barbara's, Baby said, "I'm going for a walk. Anybody want to join me?"

"Not me. I'm pooped," Rachel said, holding on to us.

"Me too," Barbara said. "That Bloody Mary did me in."

She headed out of the kitchen, snapping off her bathing suit straps as she went.

"What are you doing?" I asked, fearing she was about to take everything off.

"I don't like tan lines. Neither does Teddy. Maddy, you should know that."

"Oh-oh," Rachel said.

And to think I had actually been considering going with her. "Sweetie, anything I ever had with Teddy was a long, long time ago. And we never made it to the tan line stage, so get over it." I'd had just enough liquor that I could speak my mind.

Baby's bikini bottom was half down one hip. Barbara broke free from us and squared her shoulders. "Baby, going skinny-dipping in front of the house is one thing. But please tell me you're not thinking about walking naked as a jaybird down the beach. That is something totally different."

Baby cocked her head at Barbara, defiance lighting her eyes. "And if I did, what business is that of yours?"

"I'll tell you what business it is," I said, my slow temper flaring. "This isn't a deserted island, Baby.

You know that. The Gullahs might live on the other side, but it doesn't mean they stay there. Why do you think any of them would want to see you prancing around naked?" I was fed up with her nonsense.

"Maybe they'd like it," Baby retorted.

Rachel swung around and came close to putting a finger on Baby's chest. "You listen to me. This may be your house but it's not your show. We are the girls of August, not the tramps of August. I've changed my mind. We're going to go for a walk together, and it's going to be pleasant. And not a single damn one of us is going to take off our clothes. Your coochie stays covered. Got it?"

Baby lifted a defiant little face at us, her jawline set hard, yet still pretty. She had moxie; I appreciated that in her.

"Fine. Let me wrap up like I'm from Riyadh," she said, grabbing a beach towel off the back of a chair and wrapping it around herself so tightly she looked like a human Q-tip. "Number one, I had no plans to march down the beach naked. And number two, if I wanted to frolic nude from one end of the island to another, I damned well would do it. And there's nothing you could do to stop me. This is *my* island." She tossed back her head as though she were the queen of England, pulled the towel even tighter, and snapped, "Let's go."

*   *   *

Despite the kerfuffle with Baby, it was, all in all, a glorious first day on Tiger Island. We walked the entire island, south to north—me trying and failing to figure out where Mac's old house might once have stood—and didn't come across a single soul until we neared the northern tip, where a young black man stood alone on the beach, surf-fishing. His face looked carved from basalt, like a statue's.

"Earl!" Baby squealed, and she ran ahead of us, greeting him with a hug.

"Who in the hell do you suppose this is?" Rachel grumbled.

"They sure do appear to know each other well," Barbara said. "Look, she's holding his hand."

"He looks like he ought to be on Easter Island," I said.

"I'm glad he's on Tiger," Rachel said, and growled softly in her throat.

Baby waved us over. "Come on, come meet Earl," she hollered.

Earl, it turned out, was a Gullah fisherman from the other side of the island.

"Welcome to Tiger Island," he said. "Baby tells me it's your first time out here."

"Yes. Yes, it is," I said.

"It's a magical place. We can tell that already," Barbara said.

"You live here full-time?" Rachel asked, as if the very idea were nutty.

"Oh, yes. Me and my whole family."

"How wonderful!" Barbara said. "I wish I lived here full-time."

"But Barbara, where would you get your hair done?" Rachel teased.

"I tell you what," Earl said. "Out here, if you don't have it, you don't need it."

"That's true," Baby said, squeezing his hand.

"Now listen," Earl said. "Maybe Baby has already told you, but it's worth repeating. Don't you go in the water when it's murky. You want to see those tiger sharks coming. We don't call it Tiger Island for nothing." And then he winked at us and I had two impressions. One, I wasn't sure if he was teasing or not. And two, I thought that wink was aimed solely at Baby.

"Those little sharks wouldn't hurt a fly," Baby said, and then she started laughing as if she'd just told a whopper of a joke. She pecked Earl on the cheek. "We gotta go, sweets, but you let me know if you need me. OK? I'm serious."

"You know I will," Earl said.

We said our good-byes and headed off in the direction we'd come from. We had gone only a few feet when Rachel, pausing to pick up a honey-colored scallop shell, said under her breath, "What do you want to bet he'll need her."

If Baby heard her, she didn't let on. She simply

continued to chatter in that stream-of-consciousness way she had.

"Earl is the nicest fella. Well, next to Teddy, that is. Looks like the tide is coming in. I'm so hungry I could eat a whale. I want to find me a sand dollar. I haven't found one in a coon's age. I wish we were like the Indians and used shells as money. We'd ALL be rich then. Lookee there, down a ways, at Mr. Blue Heron. Isn't he pretty! Fishing the shallows, just like an old man. Hey, are y'all having any fun?"

"Loads," Rachel said.

"We'd have more fun if you'd..." Barbara didn't finish her sentence, which I was relieved about because I was certain she had intended to say something such as *keep your big mouth shut*.

"If I'd what?" Baby asked.

"Nothing."

"I'm going for a dip," I said, congratulating myself on how adept I was becoming at avoidance.

"Watch out for the tiger sharks!" Baby chortled, dropping the towel to the sand and plunging into the surf.

By the time we got back to Tiger's Eye, we were sunburned, famished, and exhausted. I threw together shrimp and pasta in olive oil and lemon for supper. Barbara tossed a good green salad. And Rachel made sure to pour lots and lots of pinot grigio.

We ate outside, the sea breeze whipping our hair

and tingling our sunburned skin, and we laughed as we told stories of Augusts past. The time the fish-monger came to our house and proclaimed his love for all four of us (Mississippi). And the time Barbara got confused because we'd rented a little, nonde-script house on the Florida Gulf Coast that looked like all the other nondescript houses in the neighbor-hood. After a beach stroll one afternoon, she walked into the wrong bungalow, helped herself to a Coca-Cola, and flopped down on the couch. The old cou-ple who owned the place screamed bloody murder when they opened their front door and saw Barbara sitting there like she owned the place (Longboat Key). The full moon that was so big and low over the water, Melinda burst into tears and said it was the most beautiful thing she'd ever seen (St. Si-mons Island). Hurricane George forcing us from our charming digs in Orange Beach, Alabama, on our fi-nal night, so that we moved on to Mobile and had a raucously fine hurricane party that was crashed by a contingent of young Swedish marine scientists who were studying the effects of freshwater intrusion on oyster beds. That old, run-down place on the Outer Banks with its defunct gas pump that Barbara was convinced was going to blow up, shredding us all to smithereens. The last house we shared—Melinda's final August—where we gazed at the calm Gulf and made promises to each other that we'd probably never, ever be able to keep, such as the one I made to Rachel: *I will never complain when you say something sarcastic as long as it's also funny* (St. Teresa, Florida).

"I think a return trip to St. Teresa might be in order one day," I mused.

Rachel picked at the last of her shrimp and said nothing.

Barbara, who had cleaned her plate, said, "I dunno. Might be too damn sad."

Baby sighed as though she did not want to hear Melinda's name spoken even once more and then—having eaten three helpings (where did she put it all?)—pushed herself away from the table, walked over to the hammock at the opposite end of the porch, flopped down, and said, "Awwwww. I sure wish Teddy was here," admiring the rock on her finger.

"Just ignore her," Rachel growled.

"Attention-seeking little twit," Barbara purred.

"I'm getting fed up with the Teddy this and Teddy that," I whispered.

"Looks like the floor show is about to begin." Rachel tossed down her napkin and watched as Baby pranced down the steps and began to cartwheel across the front yard, expertly missing the rugosa roses and their torturous thorns.

"Wheeeeee!"

"Baby," Barbara called, reaching for the wine bottle, "your pretty house sort of reminds me of Cornelia's home."

She did a backward somersault.

"How's that?"

"The roses," Rachel said. "The goddamned roses."

"How old is this place, Baby?" I asked.

"I think Granddaddy built it in the nineteen twenties. Or was it the thirties? I don't remember. But anyway, he's long dead. And my mama—did I tell you she's dead? Passed on almost a year ago now—gave it to me as a wedding present. I redecorated. Got rid of a lot of the old stuff. I mean, I kept some things...stuff my mama and my grandparents loved. But some of the pictures, furniture, photos, what-have-yous, I chucked." She did a split and then spun into a standing position, which led into something that resembled a backbend.

"Why?" If she would just stop moving, I thought, my growing nausea might ease. "Why would you throw away family photos?"

Indeed, she did stop for a moment. "Clean slate. I paid a family on the other side of the island to bag up all the old crap and do whatever they wanted with it. And I hired Mrs. Louise K. Baker, of Louise K. Baker Interior Designs, to fluff up the place. I think she did pretty good." Baby got on all fours and crab-walked.

"For heaven's sake," Rachel spit.

"I still don't understand. How could you get rid of family heirlooms?" Barbara asked, rising and walking over to the rail.

"Just did." Baby grunted and then collapsed in the grass. "I tried to get Teddy to take down that damn lightning rod, or at least that blue glass ball my daddy put up there. But he wouldn't do it. He will, though. Just you wait and see."

"I like that glass ball. It's pretty," I said.

"No! It's not! It's like an eyeball that watches my every move," Baby said, staring skyward.

"Well, anyway," I said, "Cornelia's house was where we first gathered, so even though none of us could stand her, that house is a part of us."

"Yep. Shit. I guess so," Rachel said.

"Wasn't that wedding something? Like a *Great Gatsby* wedding." Barbara reached over to the table, picked up her wine, and swirled it.

"Teddy and Cornelia's?" Rachel looked at Barbara as if she'd lost her marbles. "It was ridiculous."

"You could have solved world hunger with what they spent on flowers alone," I said.

"Teddy never talks about her," Baby said as she made grass angels, her arms and legs flapping against the green sod. *Somebody keeps this yard up*, I thought. *Probably one of the Gullahs*. "Is she pretty?"

I shrugged my shoulders. Barbara glanced at me

over the lip of her wineglass and rolled her eyes. Rachel said, "If you like Barbie dolls with money for blood, yeah."

The nausea that had stalked me on and off all day eased and I started laughing. Teddy might have dumped me for the Ice Queen, but I got a keeper and he got a divorce.

"Were you always a caterer? You cook good," Baby said to me, sitting up, her bikini-bottomed bum nestled in the grass.

"She's gonna get worms sitting like that," Rachel said into her glass.

"Nope," I said, and I downed a healthy gulp of pinot.

"She stopped teaching when she and Mac moved to Charleston," Rachel answered for me.

"Why?"

"Because teachers don't get paid squat in South Carolina and she followed her bliss." Barbara took a deep breath, filling herself up with the ocean breeze.

"Her what?"

"Bliss!" Rachel spun around in her chair. "B-L-I-S-S."

"Oh!" Baby crowed. "I thought she said 'piss.'"

I looked up from my wine and Rachel, Barbara, and I caught each other in a shared glance that was solid, born of old times with the promise of new ones. We all began to sputter and giggle—Baby too.

"I followed my piss!" I said between hiccupping laughter.

"She followed her piss and her dreams came true!" Rachel screamed.

"Follow your piss, Obi-Wan Kenobi," Barbara intoned.

"Ignorance is...," Baby started.

"Piss!" we all yelled.

And that's what we were doing when the first star pierced the night sky. Being silly. Laughing as loudly as we possibly could, as if we wanted God to hear.

*   *   *

Later that evening, after a round of "Good nights" and "Sleep tights," I slipped under the damp-and-salt-smelling sheets feeling more exhausted than I had a right to. Still and all, despite my bone-tiredness, sleep did not come easily. I listened to the surf crash and recede, crash and recede, and with each onslaught, thoughts of my family—my real family—washed over me. Out there, outside my closed bedroom door, when the girls and I were chatting and laughing, swimming and strolling, my real family seemed like a distant, pleasant galaxy that I soon would return to, so I gave it little thought. But when I was alone, in the dark, memories of Mac welled up and I missed him so badly my spine ached.

But he would not have fit in here, nor would any of the other spouses. Ours was a female circle and the men would have been broken links. We all knew that. Besides, it wasn't as if we didn't go on "real family" vacations. Mac and I went on at least one a year—a single trip that was huge and fabulous, and then weekend getaways as time allowed, to favored spots such as Asheville to go skiing or even Manhattan to catch a new musical. We'd been to Paris, London, Rome, Morocco. We'd sipped champagne at a café in the shadow of the Eiffel Tower. We'd cruised down the Thames in a Mississippi-style stern-wheeler. We'd kissed like passionate teenagers in St. Peter's Square as a flock of nuns from some Eastern European country looked on and giggled. I have ridden a camel, by God, in the Sahara freaking Desert. But over all the years and all the places, neither Mac nor I has ever said, "Hey, let's go spend some time by the sea. St. John. Acapulco. Hawaii." For the two of us, the sea never made it onto our radar screen. It was as though beach-side vacations were the sole realm of the girls of August and so Mac and I instinctively avoided them.

As I pulled the sheet up to my chin, I thought that perhaps I would try to change that. I conjured an image of the two of us, hand in hand, strolling along a beach that looked pretty much like Tiger Island's shore. In my imagination he kissed my lips.

"I miss you, sweetie," I whispered.

Lying there in the dark alone, I listened for an answer. And though one never came, my ears caught scraps of what was happening elsewhere in the house. I heard Barbara tossing and turning. It sounded as though she were having a wrestling match with the sheets. And then, muffled, came the sound of someone weeping. Rachel weeping. Tough-as-nails Rachel, a woman I'd rarely even seen tear up, was bawling. Oh, dear God, why? I wondered if I should go to her, but quickly thought better of it. She had her pride. My barging in would be an act of thievery.

So I lay there, listening and fretting, and then I realized that the only person who seemed absent was Baby. From her room, nothing. It was so quiet, I wondered if she was roaming the night, near naked, a moonchild, lost in her own strange innocence.

CHAPTER

4

I rose early the next morning and all was still. I made coffee and put extra cream in my mug, hoping to ease my stomach, which was threatening to revolt. I decided to let everyone sleep in as long as she wanted. After all, this was, technically, a vacation and not a how-to-have-fun boot camp.

Cup in hand, I headed outside. The sand pathway that led from the stairs to the ocean cut the sodded, extravagantly planted yard into perfect, equal halves. I thought it looked like a white stripe down an alligator's back. A zebra butterfly flitted among the roses and a hummingbird hovered over the deep throat of some sort of yellow blossom on a climbing vine. Bees buzzed all about. This was paradise. A great blue heron fished the shallows and beyond the breakers, a pod of dolphin made their way south. They were probably following a trough rich with mullet and bait-fish, I thought; and indeed, just then a mullet jumped, jumped, jumped three times, and my mouth suddenly watered at the idea of a fish fry.

But the girls of August, I thought, sipping my coffee and heading to the water's edge, *have never fished together*. Who, after all, would bait our hooks?

"Yum," I said aloud, a platter of golden fried fish blooming in my mind's eye. "I will. I'm not afraid."

Surely Baby and Teddy had fishing gear around here. Maybe even some frozen bait. What was that unidentified brick I had spied in the freezer when I was getting ice cubes last night?

A line of pelicans glided inches above the water's surface and a battalion of seagulls in their gray-and-white frock coats ventured near, probably in the hope that I had food and was in the mood to share. The sand was stippled with footprints that headed out of the yard and followed the dune line north. They were petite little prints. Baby's prints, if I had to guess. And I did not see a return set. "Interesting," I murmured, coffee mug aloft.

Maybe she had ventured into the night and encountered a wild pig. Or that Earl fellow. They were awfully friendly with each other. But would she cheat on Teddy? This soon? I turned away from the footprints and gazed out at the Atlantic, but it didn't give up any secrets. Mac was probably already at work, seeing his first patient, telling him or her to say, "Aaaaaah." He loved being a family practitioner. He didn't make as much money as the other guys—Oliver the oncologist; Hugh the heart surgeon; Teddy the pediatric surgeon—but we did all right. And we were steady. Good together. The surf bubbled over my feet and for a moment I felt as though it were sweeping me back to Charleston and Mac, something I both wanted and didn't. I sipped the last of my coffee and headed up to the house to see what the girls were doing and perhaps get a head start on my fishing idea. At the dune line, I paused and placed my foot—a size eight on a good day—next to what I estimated to be a diminutive size-six footprint, a faint worry rising inside me. I hoped nothing bad had happened to crazy Baby.

*   *   *

Barbara sat at the kitchen table, her face buried in an ice pack.

"What happened to you?" I asked, pouring another cup of coffee.

"Couldn't sleep. Hangover," she murmured into the washcloth that encased the ice cubes. Then she moaned.

"Coffee?"

"Uh-huh."

"You know what's good for that, don'tcha?"

She pulled the ice pack away and looked at me, her platinum streaks falling across her face. "Hair O'Dog."

"That," I said, sliding a steaming mug her way, "and a day spent surf-fishing!"

"Oh, fuck you," she said. "Do I look like I even know which end of a fish to eat?"

"Fishing doesn't require such knowledge."

"You're joking, right?"

I shook my head no. She slumped, resting her head in her hands. Then she sat back up, reached for her coffee, and, as if I weren't there, stared out the window, her face trembling before it went still. Sad and still. And I realized that yesterday's merry demeanor had been a facade and that the tossing and turning and inability to sleep were fueled by something more than having imbibed with a tad too much enthusiasm. I sipped my coffee but kept my eyes on her.

*   *   *

After Barbara excused herself to take a shower, I went in search of fishing paraphernalia. I decided the garage behind the house would be my best bet. "Garage," however, was an inadequate name for the building because it was, indeed, a diminutive and detailed copy of the big house. It even sported a small widow's walk topped with a shrunken replica of the lightning rod. The hand-painted sign above the door indicated that this was "Tiger's Third Eye." *There are fishing rods in there*, I thought, gazing at the sign. *I just know it.*

Hoping that no one had done something silly and equipped the place with a security alarm, I pushed open the door and entered. A ghost crab skittered out. The scent of salt and musty air rolled over me, feeding my near-constant companion, nausea. I stepped inside and paused, allowing my eyes to adjust to the relative darkness.

The room slowly bloomed into focus, and I was mightily impressed at what I saw. Behold: a masterwork of organization. I did not believe Baby had had a hand in the precision before me because such perfection required rigid discipline with a dose of obsessive-compulsive disorder thrown in. Hell, I wasn't even sure if Teddy was capable of this sort of clockwork tidiness.

Built-in shelves and organizing nooks complete with labels so that nothing would be misplaced were neatly filled with everything it took to run a house such as Tiger's Eye and enjoy what the island had to offer. Cleaning supplies, extra everything (including plastic bags, trash bags, toilet paper, cupcake liners, and bug spray), outdoor eating paraphernalia, surfboards and bodyboards, fishing rods, hooks, pliers, buckets, two refrigerators stocked with beer, and one freezer filled with a fisherman's delight: bait shrimp, finger mullet, and ice. Teddy didn't know squat about marrying the right girl, but he had a knack, even a passion, for fishing. I suspected he loved Tiger's Eye with a vigor that rivaled any lust he held for Baby.

I gathered everything we would need and put most of it in a rolling cart, including one cooler for fish, one for drinks and nibbles, and a small one for bait. As I leaned the rods against the side of the house, Baby strolled up wrapped in nothing but a sarong, her bikini, and the skin God gave her.

"Well. Look what the cat dragged in."

She ignored me so I tried again. "Hey, Baby, where have you been? Were you out all night?" Her hair was full of knots and from the circles under her eyes, it looked as if she hadn't slept a wink. She gained the steps and waved me off. "Hey, Baby, I'm talking to you."

"What do you want?" She stood on the porch and stared at the ceiling fan.

"Where were you last night?"

"It's none of your business."

Well, she had certainly gotten up on the wrong side of somebody's bed. "I don't think wandering around alone at night is the best idea."

"For your information, Maddy, I wasn't wandering. What are you doing, anyway?"

"We're fixing to go fishing." And even though I didn't want to bother with her sassy self, I also didn't think it was right to leave her out. "You game?"

"Sure. Why not." She flung open the front door, bumped into Rachel, who was on her way out, and slammed it shut.

"What the hell was that about?" Rachel asked, looking behind her and then eyeing the rods.

"I have no idea. Nor do I care."

Rachel was clear-eyed, showing no sign of last night's tear-storm. She was showered and fresh, with a different bathing suit on from yesterday's green number. This one was black and sexy with a jewel glinting between her boobs. She nodded at the rods. "Really?"

"Oh yeah. I'm setting us up right out there, in front of the house, close to booze and bathrooms. Easy-weezie."

"All right," she said, biting her lower lip, "but I promise you, if I catch a shark, somebody is going to have hell to pay."

"You might catch a baby shark," I said, hoisting rods in one hand and a bucket in the other, "but a big guy would break the rod or snap the line before you could bring it in."

"Sort of like *cut bait and run*," Rachel murmured, staring at the ocean.

"What?"

"The shark," she said, bitterness under her words, "it's always in charge." Then she bent down and grabbed the tackle box I'd set beside the cart stacked with coolers. "Fuck it. Let's do this thing."

She marched on ahead of me, her footsteps falling hard against the sand, and I got a sinking feeling that Rachel Greene was trying to stomp the life out of something.

*   *   *

Baby, as it turned out, was a good fisherman. She was confident and fearless, and it dawned on me that in addition to her youth and beauty, Teddy had probably been attracted to her skills with a rod and reel.

Barbara, on the other hand, was a mess. She landed the first fish of the morning—a red drum—but she screamed like an apoplectic schoolgirl until we unhooked it and sent it on its way.

Rachel snagged a nice-size snapper, but was uncharacteristically winded by the exertion of bringing it in, and said, as I slipped the pretty fish onto ice, "That's all for me."

I caught a couple more snapper. Mainly, though, I lost my bait to I don't know what…probably crabs and catfish.

But Baby reeled them in as if she were in a tournament. She even, for some reason, kept her sarong on and had planted an Atlanta Braves baseball cap on her pretty little head.

"How in the hell did you learn to fish like that?" Rachel asked from her prone position in the lounge chair she had pulled down from the house.

"All my summers were spent here," Baby answered, unhooking a catfish, successfully avoiding its barbs, then tossing it back into the sea with the admonition "And don't come back!" She re-baited her hook, threading it twice through a cold, dead shrimp. "You can't claim to be a Gaillard if you don't know your way around a pole."

"I'm not touching that one," Rachel growled.

Barbara, who was slowly nursing a wine cooler, having given up on any hope of catching a fish, said to Baby, "You really *are* from here. Flat-out crazy."

Baby shot Barbara an if-looks-could-kill glance and then said, "Here." She held out her rod. "Use mine."

This attitude made no sense. Where had our silly Baby gone? "If she doesn't want to fish she doesn't have to," I said.

"Stay out of it, Maddy," she snapped, keeping her gaze on Barbara. "Come on. Up. I'll teach you how."

Barbara lowered her sunglasses and looked first at me, then at Rachel. We both shrugged our shoulders.

"You're on your own this time, Barbara," Rachel

said in her deep, smoky voice. "I'm going for a swim." She stood, headed down the beach until, I suppose, she felt she was out of the reach of any wildly flung lines, and waded into the surf.

"Let me see your fishing stance," Baby ordered.

Barbara stared at the rod as if it were a staff covered in snakes. "What do you mean?"

"Pretend. You've already cast and the line is in the water. How do you hold this thing?"

Barbara cleared her throat. It was evident that Baby wasn't going to let up. Barbara gripped the rod tighter and then held the rod in front of her with the end pointing downward.

"No. Lift it up. It's a fishing rod. And you need to keep your finger here." Baby adjusted Barbara's grip. "Real light on the line. That way you'll feel what's happening out there. Under the water."

Barbara tightened her mouth and I surmised she was weighing two options: let Baby teach her, or tell Baby to shove it. She settled on the former. "OK. But you cast it for me."

"No," Baby said, emphasizing the vowel. "I'm teaching *you*!" She shook her head as if disgusted.

"Fine," Barbara spit. She marched into the water, ankle-deep, and cast her rod perfectly. Except no line was released. "What the hell happened?"

I started laughing as I baited my hook.

"You have to release the bale. Look. Watch me."

Baby grabbed the rod, executed a flawless cast, and handed it back to her. "Here."

Baby walked over to the cooler, fished out a Bud Light, flopped down in the lounge chair, expertly shimmied her sarong down to her hips, and said, her barely sheathed boobs aimed at the sun, "Let me know if you need me."

*   *   *

Our first indication that Barbara had had a strike was her shrieking, "Oh my God! Oh my God! Oh my God!"

Baby, who had dozed off with the Bud bottle between her legs, opened her eyes in a flash and said, "What?"

"I've got something! I've got something big!"

"Probably a stingray," Rachel called from down the beach.

I looked at the rod. It was bending pretty good. Not a stingray.

"What do I do? What do I do? What do I do?" she shouted.

"Let loose on the tension," Baby said, running to aid Barbara, the sarong falling down around her ankles. She ran out of it, and nothing on that fine body of hers jiggled. It was enough to make a middle-aged woman cry.

Baby fiddled with the tension and then shouted in-

structions: "Let it run. Exhaust it. This is a slow game
and you're gonna win!" A Little League–coach gleam
brightened her eyes.

And Barbara? She actually looked jazzed. I mean,
really jazzed. Not fake merry, but loose and happy,
as if this exercise in the visceral and primal act of
taking the life of one of nature's creatures had un-
leashed in her a warrior goddess. She cut first left,
then right in tandem with the movements of the underwater question mark. That old Hemingway line
came to mind: *Grace under pressure.*

"It fits you," I yelled over the surf roar.

"What does?"

"The battle."

"You have no idea!" And she started reeling in her
catch.

*   *   *

As it turned out, Barbara landed a redfish. A big one.
Baby claimed it was just under the legal limit. But I
suspected it might have been a centimeter or so over.
Barbara was beaming. We took a picture of her holding it at just about breast level, her hair swept up in
a cascading ponytail and her sunglasses sliding down
her long, thin nose. I could tell the poor dead crea-
ture made her a tad squeamish, but her pride at having
landed it gave her the courage to boast.

"My kids aren't going to believe this!" she said.

"Hugh isn't going to believe it," I said.

"He'll say it was all staged," Rachel chimed in.

"What do I do with it?"

"We're going to put it in the fish cooler with the snapper and then we're going to have one hell of a fish fry!" I was pleased as punch that my early-morning vision was about to be realized.

Everyone pitched in. I had to hand it to Baby. She not only knew how to fish, she knew how to scale and fillet them too. Rachel made a to-die-for cucumber salad with dry dill and cream. Barbara, who'd gotten a second wind thanks to the hair of the dog and her triumph over the redfish, made a pitcher of mojitos, muddling mint she'd brought with her from her home garden. I went all out, fixing hush puppies, corn salad, and black bean caviar. I hummed a tune whose name I didn't know as I dredged the fish in cornmeal spiked with a touch of cayenne.

We ate outside and laughed and told secrets and lies. Barbara said that Hugh had a third nipple, a little number down near the bottom of his rib cage.

"Do you suck on it?" Rachel asked.

"Oh, hell no." Barbara emphatically shook her head and tightened her grip around her glass.

"What?" Baby asked, scrunching her face. "You can't have a third nipple. That's freaky."

"Well. It's not a full-blown nipple," Barbara said,

as if that explained everything. "Did you know," she asked, leaning forward and pointing with her fork, "that men can actually lactate?"

"What's that?" Baby asked in a tone of voice that suggested she had already decided that whatever lactation was, it had to be the grossest thing on the planet.

"Puh-lease," Barbara said. "You know, milk, as in nursing."

Baby looked at us with her pouty mouth hung open. She was not getting it.

"You know when women have a baby?" I asked her, wondering why I, the childless one, was explaining this.

"Yeah."

"They have breast milk. You've heard of that?"

Baby rolled her eyes. Evidently she thought we were the stupid ones.

"That's called *lactation*," I said in a steady, even voice. I didn't want her to think I was talking down to her.

Baby scratched her neck and looked up at the porch ceiling, pondering. Then she tapped her index finger on the table and said to Rachel, "You mean to tell me that men have breast milk? I don't think so."

Rachel stone-faced her. "Baby, you just suck on Teddy's nipples long enough—it might take you days or weeks, but I suspect you're up to the job—and you will eventually find yourself with a mouth full of Teddy milk."

"Ewwww!" I said, and my stomach lurched.

"That is fucking disgusting," Barbara said, swirling her drink.

"You all are crazy," Baby said, crossing her arms in front of her.

Rachel smiled triumphantly. She had won.

"Does anyone want seconds?" I asked, changing the subject.

Barbara caught my eye and nodded in the direction of the beach. Earl was approaching from the north.

"I want a wee bit more of that redfish," Rachel said, poking around at the platter.

"These hush puppies are great," Baby said, stuffing her mouth with a whole one, and then she saw him too. With her mouth full, she said, "I'll be right back." She stood, adjusted her sarong so that it tied around her neck, and walked down the path to greet him.

"What the hell is going on?" Barbara asked.

"She's already cheating on Teddy. I'd bet my bottom dollar." .

"I don't think so," I said.

"Why not? Look at her." Rachel glared in Baby's direction.

"Just a hunch." They were in an animated conversation and neither of them was smiling. "She didn't come home last night."

"She what!" Barbara's eyes flashed in the fading light.

"Why didn't you tell us?"

"Well, where the hell was she?" Barbara pushed back her plate, picked up her drink.

"She wouldn't tell me. Said it was none of my business."

"Why that little bitch," Rachel said. "I almost feel sorry for Teddy."

Baby rose to her tiptoes and kissed Earl's cheek.

"I have half a mind to tell him just as soon as we get back to the mainland."

"Barbara," I said, "we don't know what's going on. It could be anything."

Rachel let out a rueful laugh. "Yeah, like what?"

I shrugged, sipped my drink. I watched Baby wipe the side of her face, as though she were wiping away a tear. "I dunno. I mean, basically she grew up out here. For all we know, Earl is her half brother."

"Ha! I'll believe that when pigs fly," Barbara said, pouring herself another drink.

I wanted to say, "Ease up on the booze, Babs," but thought better of it. There was already enough antagonism in the air. And in a bid to slide us back into vacation mode, I made a suggestion. "You know what?"

Rachel and Barbara didn't respond. I think they were pondering Baby's situation and hoping, to varying degrees, that she actually was doing something untoward.

"The dishes can wait. Let's go lie down in the surf like a pod of beached whales. What do you think?"

Rachel shrugged. "What the fuck. What else are we going to do out here?" She stood and said, "Barbara, bring the wine. We'll just suck straight from the bottle."

"That sure as hell is better than sucking on Hugh's third nipple," Barbara said, laughing.

"I guess so," I agreed. "Why oh why did you tell us that!"

We made our way down to the shore, satiated, slightly looped, simmering with curiosity. When I looked, Earl was heading back the way he'd come. Baby wandered over. She was quiet and reserved, and something about her demeanor kept us from prying. She looked over her shoulder. When Earl was out of sight, she took off her sarong, adjusted her bikini without any modesty whatsoever, and lay with us.

*   *   *

That night, I did not know if Barbara was restless or if Rachel wept or if Baby stole away in the moonlight. Rather, I paid attention to my own self, sleeping like the dead but dreaming of the living. Mac and I were elated over something. We didn't talk about it because words might have diminished our joy. He held me sweet and tight, and we floated over Tiger Island, cocooned in the velvet canvas of the sky. Eventually, we became our own star.

CHAPTER

5

On our third full day on Tiger Island we, each of her own volition, fell into the ease and isolation of the place. We lolled about, doing essentially nothing. I read a trashy dime-store novel I plucked from Baby's library. Barbara sunbathed and worked on sudoku puzzles. Rachel sat in the shade and scribbled in a note pad she had brought with her. Baby disappeared and returned. She set up a jigsaw puzzle on a tile-topped wrought-iron table in the sun-room. She hid the box so we wouldn't know what we were working on, saying that it was the only fair way. I put together two corners on my way to the bathroom. Someone else began fitting together pieces of sky. We swam, we walked, we napped. We were quieter than before. And when we gathered for dinner—I thawed out steaks I had brought with me and grilled them in

the front yard, the sea breeze ruffling my hair, the
dream hanging over me with a sweetness I had not
expected—we talked about the turtle nest Rachel had
found about a mile south of the house, and Barbara
said she had always wanted to visit Venice and hoped
her kids would go with her if she ever made it that far,
and Baby said out of nowhere that she didn't think
God should let babies die.

"Why would you say such a sad thing?" I asked.

"No reason. Sometimes I think about stuff. That's
all."

Rachel started to say something but stopped. Then
cocked her head at Baby and asked, "Does Teddy
know you know all those Gullahs on the other side of
the island?"

"Of course he does," Baby said, her face clear as a
summer blue sky. "Why wouldn't he know?"

Barbara laughed a bitter, short laugh. "Yeah, I bet,"
she whispered loudly enough for us to hear.

"You know what, Barbara?" Baby stood and tossed
back her hair.

"What?" Barbara slurred a bit.

"I think you're just jealous. You ain't got this."
Baby pointed at her body. "You ain't got nothing
natural"—she flipped Barbara's hair—"and you
couldn't hang on to a man like Teddy if your life de-
pended on it. And by the way"—she glared at all of
us—"somebody needs to put up the fishing gear ex-

actly as I had it. It feels as if I've spent half my life organizing this place and it's going to stay that way." She grabbed her beach towel, turned on her heel, held up one arm, shot us a bird, and marched down the beach.

"Hold on one minute," Barbara cried, jumping from her chair.

I grabbed her arm. "Don't."

"Don't what?"

"Don't go after her."

"Listen to me." Barbara jerked away. Tears filmed her eyes but they did not fall. "I will do any fucking thing I want. Including kicking that little tramp's ass."

She looked at us and her lips trembled. I think they were holding back a torrent of words, of secrets. But the dam held. "Just forget it!" she said and then stomped into the house. A few moments later, we heard her bedroom door slam.

I looked at Rachel, who simply shrugged and poked absentmindedly at her mesclun salad.

"What in the world is eating her?"

"Who knows? It could be anything," Rachel said, aiming her fork at a cherry tomato.

"Aren't you concerned? I mean, she's been drinking like a fish. So far, this week has been one long bender. Something is wrong!"

Rachel looked up from her plate, her eyes hooded with her heavy lids. "Maddy."

"What?"

"Quit trying to fix everything."

She speared the tomato, held it aloft, studied it for a moment, set it down, shoved back her chair, and walked away, down the beach in the opposite direction Baby had taken, enveloped in the day's dying light, her shoulders slouched, signaling sadness or defeat. I didn't know which.

I looked out to sea, at the push and pull of the incessant surf. The wind was picking up, the tide rising. Storm clouds burgeoned along the horizon, pulsing with lightning as though the clouds were seizing, convulsing. So Baby was the organizer of the house. Who would have thought it? And Barbara was threatening to career out of control. As I mulled over those two surprising revelations, a strange and unreasonable fear crept into my bones. What would we do if the storm remained out there forever and a day, relentlessly blistering the sky, threatening for all eternity to come ashore?

*   *   *

I was sunk in a deep sleep—the sort of sleep in which if you did dream, you would never remember it—when a window-shaking clap of thunder roused me and, though my lids were closed, I was aware that an ungodly bright flash had split the darkness. I bolted upright, surrounded by the pulse of repeated lightning strikes, and remembered Fossey Pearson's warning about the intensity of the recent nighttime storms. I threw back the covers, got out of bed, and checked on the others.

Rachel's bed was empty. The storm must have roused her too. But Barbara and Baby remained magically unaware, unruffled by the clamorous weather. The wind whipped at the clapboard and I feared that we were in the grip of a sudden hurricane. But surely they would have evacuated us. No one would allow four women and a handful of Gullahs to perish.

"It's just a bad, garden-variety blow," I whispered to myself as I wandered the house in search of Rachel. The jigsaw puzzle had one more completed block, but I still couldn't tell what the picture was. No signs of life in the kitchen. The bathrooms were empty. Living room: nothing. Library: nothing. Damn it. Was she crazy enough to be outside in this mess?

Reluctantly, but having little choice, I ventured onto the front porch. The howling wind was cold and thick with stinging grains of sand. The rain swept sideways along the porch and it, too, stung as though bursting with electrical current. Shivering, I rubbed my arms. Remaining dry was out of the question. Lightning crackled again, jagged, luminous, striking the wet sand. Thunder roared, echoing across the

ocean. Afraid, wet, ~~miserable, I drew in my breath.~~
Where was she?

"Rachel!" I called, but the wind whipped her name
right back at me. I inched over to the porch rail and
hung on. I tried to shield my face as I searched. I
scanned the beach to no avail. I gazed into the pulsing
darkness and the tumultuous sea. There. Right there,
in the boiling surf, in water up to her waist, Rachel
stood naked. She raised her arms to the sky and threw
back her head. Even from this distance, I could see by
her contorted face that she was crying.

I called her name again and ran down the porch
and across the beach, down to the water. We might
both die out here, but at least no one would ever
be able to accuse me of not trying to save her. A
wave nearly knocked her over, and Earl's comment
about the tiger sharks in a murky sea flashed through
my mind. I looked at the raging surf and then at
Rachel. She had steadied herself and was gazing too
intently into the darkness. I feared she meant to allow
the ocean to take her. I had no choice, sharks or no
sharks. I waded out and grabbed her by the waist.

"Rachel, honey, what in the world!"

She turned around, dropped her arms, and didn't
move. "Come on, baby," I said. "Come with me."

Rachel wailed. It was a child's sound. I ferried her
toward the shore, feeling as though I were guiding
not a living, breathing person but an armful of scat-

tered bones. I led her back to the porch and, in the now ebbing storm, threw a towel around her shoulders, held her, rocking her, until her sobs subsided and all the thunder was silent.

"What is it? What's going on, Rachel?" I pushed a strand of wet hair off her forehead.

"I didn't want anyone to know." She covered her face with her hands and wept.

"Tell me, Rachel. Do you understand? Please. Tell me."

She nodded yes but kept her face shrouded behind her trembling fingers. "I have cancer," she whispered, "Left breast. It's in my ovaries now." She lowered her hands and stared past me, all her fierceness gone. "There's nothing anyone can do about it."

"Of course they can do something. They can always do something."

I held her by the shoulders, and my deepest desire in the whole world at that very moment was to shake some sense into her.

"No. Maddy." She looked me in the eyes. "I waited too long. Me, a pediatric nurse. Oliver, a freaking oncologist. I just ignored the signs. Not me, nuh-uh, never me."

"Oh, dear God, Rach." I reached for her hand, the enormity of what she'd just revealed not completely sinking in. "Are you in pain?"

She shook her head. "Not yet. It doesn't hurt yet."

She looked at the ocean and whispered, "I just wanted...I just wanted to stop it before it did. Before I put the kids and Oliver through all the shit people go through when they watch somebody they love die."

"Oh, honey, no, no, no. There has got to be an answer. What does Oliver say?"

Rachel wiped her nose with the back of her hand. She lowered her head and mumbled, "He doesn't know yet."

"What? Oh, God, Rach! You have to tell him. He's a specialist. This is his field. He'll know what to do!"

Rachel sighed deeply and then looked at me again. "Madison McCauley, how long have we known each other?"

"Goodness. It's going on twenty-five years."

"Right. And in that time have you ever known me not to be a fighter?"

I shook my head no and then I began to weep.

"There ain't nothing nobody can do about this. Surgery couldn't get it all. So I'm going to need you. And when I get back, I will tell Oliver. And together, we will tell our kids. But for now...well...for now, I need this time with us together. I need it real bad."

"Then what was that about?" I nodded toward the beach.

Rachel shook her head.

"Fuck it, Maddy. I don't know. I guess I just got scared."

"Please don't do it again," I whispered.

Rachel moved her gaze to the now quiet horizon. I knew she wasn't going to answer. She wasn't a woman who made promises she couldn't keep.

*   *   *

After we went inside and dried off and slipped into fresh pajamas, we met downstairs. I had insisted. No one tries what Rachel did and then is left on her own. Not when I'm in the house. And I admit, I stood outside her bedroom and listened for all the right sounds—the closet door closing, the whirr of the hair dryer, the footsteps heading toward the door. And you can bet I made it to the living room before she did. I didn't want her to know I was keeping tabs.

I was standing by the fireplace, pretending to study the Gaillard family photo gallery, when Rachel descended the stairs.

"You know what I need?" she asked, her hand gripping the ornate oak newel post.

Her eyes had lost the frantic light of panic. Now they were calm and beginning to swell from all those tears.

"What's that?" I went to her and hugged her close.

"One of your famous hot buttered rums."

That actually sounded perfect. "OK then. Two buttered rums coming right up!"

And then, because I was a good friend, I was about to insist with foot-stomping vigor that hope was not lost. I was about to say, "Listen, Rachel, this thing isn't over yet. Do not give up."

But perhaps because she sensed what was coming, she beat me to the pass. "Madison McCauley," she said, "you have to promise me something. No one knows unless I tell them."

"What are we talking about?"

"Tonight. The cancer. Everything. Deal?"

There was no way around it. I had to agree. And I could not betray her. As much as I wanted to get us off this island at that very moment and get her to Oliver with all his knowledge about cancer, I had to honor her wishes.

"Deal."

She disappeared down the hall to use the downstairs bathroom and I went into the kitchen and gathered up what I needed. Butter, dark rum, brown sugar. I searched the cupboard and was surprised to find my secret weapon: nutmeg. I went about the preparations as if nothing had happened, as if the world were intact. But as I ran the water and poured the rum and lit the stove and monitored how long she'd been gone, there was no doubt in my mind, my heart, my soul: The world as we knew and loved it was over.

*   *   *

Tuesday arrived with blue skies that belied the tempest that had scourged us only hours before. And Rachel seemed back to her old gruff, teasing self. As she breezed past me in the kitchen, I handed her a cup of coffee. She winked at me, as if knowledge of her imminent death were a sweet secret we shared, and then plopped down at the table, saying, "Gawd. I could have slept fifty more hours. Why are you always the early bird, Maddy?"

I knew I would not breach her confidence, but I also knew that until we got off this island and she told her husband and children, I would carry the knowledge of her illness as if it were the weight of the world. Perhaps it was. At any rate, from her demeanor—it reflected no hint of doom—I knew the subject between us was closed. At least for now. "Because somebody has to keep this troop of Amazons fed," I said.

"Bacon! I want bacon!" Barbara yelled as she rounded the corner. "That's what my kids say every Sunday morning."

"Is that what you want?" I asked.

"You bet."

"You got it, sleepyhead," I said.

"What does she have?" Baby yelled from the living room. She bounced into the kitchen, curls damp, skin scrubbed and glistening. "I am sooooo hungry! Can you make pancakes?" She pecked me on the cheek.

Surprised, I pulled away and moved over to the

sink, where I grabbed a sponge and stared out the window. The world looked washed clean. And with three cheerful women on my hands, it appeared that the storm had washed clean their sorrows, fears, and other inner malaises as well.

Baby held her arms out from her sides and spun. "It's gonna be a beautiful day, mothers!"

I turned around. Whom was she talking to?

"Mothers!" Barbara's eyes flashed wide as she watched Baby spin.

"Yes! Mother, mother, mother!" She pointed to each one of us on *mother*, saving me for last.

Rachel shot us a look that clearly said, *What the fuck?*

I shrugged. No use even trying to figure out this child. "OK, you want pancakes. Who else?"

Barbara and Rachel raised their hands.

"Pancakes! Yay!" Baby shrilled and she jumped up and down three times. I thought suddenly that she must be ADD. That, or she was on drugs. Dear God.

"Don't forget the bacon. In fact, I can make it." Barbara, I noticed, had turned a soft shade of amber under all this sun.

"No you won't. Too many cooks in the kitchen."

"Great! Then I'll make the mimosas." Barbara headed to the fridge, retrieved two bottles of champagne and a carton of orange juice, closed the door with a bump of her hip, and then said, "Shoot!"

"What is it, Mother?" Baby hung a casual arm around Barbara's shoulder.

Barbara flinched and moved out of range. "I forgot to bring the champagne flutes I bought for us. They're the cutest things. The stems look like palm trees. They're cut crystal and everything."

"Palm trees!" Baby carolled. "How cool is that! I've never seen anything like that. But no problem, Mother." She shot into the pantry and yelled, "We keep a stash of champagne glasses in here. They're not fancy, but who cares!"

"What is wrong with her?" Rachel whispered.

"I don't know." I grabbed a paring knife, plucked an apple from the fruit bowl, and started to peel.

"She's plumb out of her mind," Barbara said, tapping her temple.

"Hey, Baby," Rachel called, "while you're in there, see if you can find your stash of Ritalin."

"Riddle what?" Baby appeared at the doorway of the pantry, holding four cobalt-blue champagne stems. I realized that I had mistaken her hot-pink, spaghetti-strap sundress for a T-shirt.

I stared down at the honeyed skin, and silently lectured myself that young women were different these days. They flaunted their bodies. And maybe that was OK. But if she had been my daughter...

"Never mind," Rachel said. "Just fix me a goddamned mimosa and hold the OJ."

"Yes, ma'am, Mother!" Her voice spiraled and I felt my hand tighten on the knife. As she prattled about how drunk she and Teddy had gotten on their wedding night, I closed my eyes. Apple pancakes. Not murder. Apple pancakes. Not murder. Apple pancakes...

*　　*　　*

Baby prattled nonstop through breakfast, hopping through subjects like a jackrabbit on speed. *And then when I was seven my parents sent me to a private school. I do not know what the big deal is about Kim Kardashian and her fake butt. Once you start faking things, you should not be allowed on the news. Teddy says that if he can get away over Christmas, we're going to go to Montserrat, wherever that is, but I think I'd just like to come here. Mothers, do you think I ought to have a baby now or wait a couple of years?*

"What is it with this 'mother' shit?" Rachel snapped, tossing down her napkin as though she were getting ready to rumble.

Baby, who was licking syrup off her fingers, paused and said brightly, "Because you all are mothers. And you are all old enough to be mine!" She belly-laughed and slapped the table. Again, the question hung in the air: What in the hell was wrong with her?

"Well, Baby," I said, my voice rising an octave even though I was working hard at holding myself together. "I'm not."

"Sure you are," Baby said, continuing to lick her fingers. "Wait! Oh, I get it." Her eyes gleamed with newfound knowledge. "*You* mean you don't have any kids. But you're still old enough to be my mama!" She jumped to her feet and started spinning again, showing her thong underwear the full 360.

"Baby!" Rachel snapped.

"Yes, Mother?"

"Enough with the mother stuff. Make yourself useful and clear this table and then help Barbara and me clean the kitchen."

Baby snapped to attention, clicking her heels, and saluted—stiff, tall, chest out. "Yes, Mother. Right away, Mother." And then she giggled again.

Barbara closed her eyes and shook her head. Baby didn't seem to care or notice. She stacked the dishes, jabbering away about an old boyfriend who'd had a nervous condition that got so bad he lost all his hair.

"How the hell old was *he*?" Rachel asked.

"Grandpappy old, most likely," Barbara retorted. "Hell, Teddy is probably young enough to be the old boyfriend's grandbaby."

"That's not funny!" Baby said. After a couple of silent moments during which I thought she might slide into a snit, she burst into a convulsive peal of laughter. "Oh, oh, oh my gawd! Young enough to be Geoffrey's grandbaby!" She slapped her leg and guffawed. "That is soooooo funny!"

Barbara and Rachel both rolled their eyes and Rachel poured more champagne. Baby snatched the plates off the table and headed to the sink, giggling all the way.

I left the kitchen and headed upstairs to change into my bathing suit and sit for a few minutes in blessed silence. I hadn't even gained the first riser when I heard her say, "You know, Mothers, Geoffrey was only twenty-two when he went stark, raving bald…"

*   *   *

When I finally ventured back downstairs, I found that the kitchen was spotless, Barbara and Rachel were gathering drinks, towels, snacks, and sunscreen for what promised to be a long day in the sun, and Baby was sitting at the kitchen table stacking packets of Sweet'n Low into diminutive towers while singing a song in a foreign language I couldn't identify.

I caught Barbara's eye and she mouthed, "Help me."

Rachel looked over the top of her big Jackie O sunglasses and said, "Baby, this is your mother talking. Stop playing around and go put on your damned bathing suit."

"Huh?" Baby feigned surprise, slapped her hands on her hips. "Oh, Mother, must you be such a bore!" And then she returned the sweetener packets to their container and marched upstairs to her bedroom, singing all the while. When she came back down, much to our relief, she was subdued.

But relief was destined not to last long. We could not have been seaside for more than an hour when Baby jumped from her lounge chair like a bottle rocket. "Come on, y'all," she chirped. "This is perfect weather for birthday suits! Take 'em off. God made your birthday suits. Now wear 'em! Let's go skinny-dipping!"

"He made swimsuits too," Barbara growled. She stood, her paperback fell onto the sand, and she didn't bother picking it up. "I'm going to go lie down. I feel one of my migraines coming on."

I watched Barbara make her way back to the house, staggering a little. I considered going after her but decided I should just let her rest and get her bearings. Maybe she'd fall asleep and sober up.

"For God's sake, Baby," Rachel snapped, "nobody is going skinny-dipping and don't you dare take off your swimsuit. I swear, you are behaving as if you are a hyperactive six-year-old. How does Teddy stand it?"

Baby actually stomped her foot. "He stands it because we love each other. And yes, I'm ADD. And yes, I misplaced my meds. But I'm still a good person," she screamed.

"Sit!" Rachel ordered.

And Baby did. She pouted and fumed, but eventually she ran out of steam and fell asleep under the hot, heavy sun.

"Zach behaved just like that when he was a toddler," Rachel said, rummaging through her beach tote. "But, of course, like most children, he grew out of it."

"You asked the twenty-five-thousand-dollar question. How does Teddy stand it?" I reached for my tumbler of ice water and realized that I almost felt sorry for him.

"You know what?" Rachel shook her head as she gazed at the ocean. "With the notable exception of Melinda, all that man has ever really done is think about tail and chase tail."

"Well," I said, pressing the cold, sweating tumbler to my cheek, "he didn't get any from me."

"And look how long you lasted," Rachel said.

I chuckled. She was right about that. And I was grateful that I'd never slept with him. I'm not sure that we'd all be friends if things had gone that far with Teddy and me.

"You know, I think I might go back to the house," I said. "The sun is starting to get to me."

"Let's go for a dip first. Sure cure for sunstroke."

I almost said no, but then I looked at Rachel's calm, open face—it still belied last night's terror—and I thought, *I want to spend every last second I can with you.*

Arm in arm, we waded into the water. "I love you, Madison McCauley. Don't you ever forget that," Rachel said as a wave slapped our thighs.

"I love you too, Rachel Greene. You know what?"

"What?"

"We're going to have to find her meds."

"Yep."

Rachel slipped away from me and dove below the surface. When she emerged, she was on her back, gazing at the sky. "Ahhh," she murmured, "what a beautiful day."

*   *   *

Baby might have dozed off to sleep in a snit, but she woke up equable and sweet-tempered. She seemed, I don't know, almost mature. Her mood swings made me believe that in addition to the ADD, her hormones were probably raging.

As we gathered our belongings before hiking back up to the house, I whispered to Rachel, "You get her in a game of cards, and I'll search her room."

They sat at the kitchen table, arguing over whether to play gin rummy or poker. Baby won. Gin rummy it was, and a sleepy-eyed but sober Barbara joined them.

I went upstairs and tiptoed into Baby's room. I scanned quickly. Her pills were nowhere in sight. I eased open her top dresser drawer. There, amid scant silk panties, were two Reese's Peanut Butter Cups, a plethora of scrunchies, and a worn-edged hot-pink journal. Unable to squelch my nosiness, I pulled it out and scanned its pages.

Doodles were interspersed between inspirational sayings handwritten in loopy script. "Don't walk. Dance" was sandwiched between "It is in our darkest moments that we must struggle to see the light—Aristotle (Onassis, the other Greek)" and "I can't change the direction of the wind, but I can adjust my sails to always reach my destination—Jimmy Dean (sausage master and singer)." Two pages were filled with Arabic script; it looked as if she'd been practicing penmanship. And then there was this, which made my heart break: "Dear Mommy, I miss you more than life itself. I wish I had been a better daughter. If I could do it all over again, maybe you'd still be alive. All my love, Baby."

What on earth? I closed the journal, returned it to its nest amid the panties and candy, spied a prescription bottle on the floor—it had rolled under the bed—retrieved it and set it on the dresser so that it was impossible to miss, and wondered what had happened that made Baby think she'd been a bad daughter. Surely she wasn't responsible for her mother's death. Or was she?

*   *   *

After dinner we sat around a beach fire Rachel and Barbara had made and talked about this and that... old flames, old houses, old jobs, old and discarded dreams, old favored books, long-loved movie stars. Baby stayed right there with us, bundled up in a too-big sweater and too-tight jeans, turning her face to listen to each one of us as we spoke. Saying little but apparently absorbing whatever we offered, she sometimes nodded, as if agreeing with us. She was so still and silent that I knew for sure she had found her meds. To be honest, I liked this quiet, more thoughtful Baby. And I hoped she would stick around.

At one point, after the fire had taken on a steady life and the moon had sailed far across the sky, the subject turned to movies in which the actresses so inhabited their roles that we remembered them years after we'd seen the films.

"Meryl Streep in *The Deer Hunter*," said Rachel, who, we were quite sure, had seen every movie ever made since the advent of talkies. "I was a lanky teenager in braces. My parents took all of us, which

I think they ended up regretting. It was *not* a happy movie. But all I could think was Meryl, with that long, golden hair, was the most beautiful person in the world. I wanted to look just like her. Me, the dark-eyed Jew from Jersey!"

"Well, if you're talking about faces," Barbara chimed in, "what about Anjelica Huston in that movie with Jack Nicholson. What was it called?"

"*Prizzi's Honor*," Rachel said. "I loved that movie."

Barbara snapped her fingers. "Yep. That's it. Not a pretty woman, but a handsome woman. And I mean that in the best of ways."

"I just wish I had one ounce of Halle Berry's good looks. She's going to be hot when she's a hundred and five," I said.

"You've got that right," Barbara said. "I saw her on the cover of one of those supermarket tabloids last week. In a bikini. And I mean H-O-T."

We all nodded and in the light from the beach fire I thought we all looked beautiful too.

Then Barbara, perhaps the kindest of us, looked across the fire at Baby and said, "What about you? Who's your candidate for a great actress? Or one who's a major knockout?"

"Mmmmm, I'm not sure," she said, staring into the flames. "But I think maybe"—she tapped her chin with her fingers—"maybe Rooney Mara."

We looked at each other.

"Who?" Rachel asked.

"Rooney Mara," Baby repeated, looking at us as if she couldn't believe how uninformed we were. "She's really good. She's gonna be in that movie coming out about a dragon tattoo. Teddy and I saw the previews. It looks awesome."

"Never heard of her," Barbara said.

"Nope. Me neither," Rachel said. "*Rooney Mara* sounds like a man's name." And then, as if she had forgotten Baby was sitting there, she murmured, "Too bad about young people..."

"What do you mean?" Baby asked.

Rachel looked at her, and without a stitch of animosity, said, "You don't know anything. All the great things in the world escape you because your generation is only interested in what's in front of your face. It's scary."

I had no idea why Rachel was being so bullheaded.

"Hold on there," I said, trying for damage control. "I think young people simply know things we don't and vice versa."

Missing my cue, Barbara jumped in. "What do you and Teddy talk about, anyway? I mean, you've got nothing in common. For goodness' sake, your cultural references are decades apart."

Baby didn't respond, which, I grudgingly thought, was wise. I suspected she felt outnumbered, picked on, hurt, and with good cause. She kept her big-eyed gaze on the fire, and we all trailed off into an uncomfortable silence.

Finally, Barbara said, "Well, it's late. I think we best throw some sand on this fire and go to bed. How about it, Baby?"

"Yeah, yeah, sure, I'll put out the fire." She stood and grabbed the shovel that was lying in the sand beside Rachel. "You know, I've been thinking."

"What's that?" Rachel asked, standing and slapping the sand from her rear end, totally unaware that she'd insulted Baby to her face.

"I know that Maddy has been doing all the cooking because she's, well, you know, a chef. But what if I cook breakfast in the morning? Give you the morning off, Maddy."

We all looked at each other in stunned amazement. We had never even seen Baby near the stove, and I could tell that my cohorts were stifling giggles. But what was more impressive to me was that after Rachel's rude smackdown, Baby seemed intent on taking the high ground.

"Why thank you, Baby, that would be wonderful," I said.

She smiled that wide, pretty smile of hers, leaned over, and pecked my cheek. This time I did not move away. "Y'all go on to bed. I'll get this."

"You sure?" Barbara asked.

"Absolutely. Go on." She waved us into the house and we took our leave.

I looked after her. *She's not a dumb bunny, I thought. Under all that—goofiness—she's as smart as a whip. I wonder what's going on with her.*

As we entered the living room and closed the door, Rachel said, "Well good goddamn, looks like we're rubbing off on the poor little thing."

"Does she even know how to turn on the oven?" Barbara asked.

"Whether she does or doesn't," I said, "we've got to let her try. You know, she's not the enemy."

"Yeah," Rachel grumbled as she headed upstairs, "I guess we ought to be a little nicer. Damn it."

And with that we ascended the stairs, offered our good nights, and drifted off to our own rooms, where, I suppose, we each considered sleepily what the next day would bring.

As I pulled up the covers and settled into the cool sheets, my thoughts turned to Rachel, with whom I could never really be mad. In the darkness I tried to imagine what a dying woman dreamed of. I decided that she dreamed of her children.

"Her children," I whispered, and I saw her five kids—all young adults, most already in college—crowded around their dying mom. All were weeping. That was the last thought I had before sleep took me.

*   *   *

I was roused from a velvet sleep the next morning by sweet, sweet old-fashioned scents that drew me out of bed and down the hall, where I bumped into Rachel and Barbara, who, it would seem, had smelled them too.

We ran barefoot down the stairs like kids on Christmas morning. We hushed each other as we tiptoed across the living room. We peeked into the kitchen and could barely believe our eyes: Baby hard at work, her polka-dot bikini barely hanging on. Her face was scrunched in concentration as she stirred something on the stove. She appeared to be immersed in adult thought. It was an arresting sight.

"Mmmmmmmm," Barbara said in a hushed tone, lifting her face to the scents of oatmeal, sugar, vanilla, raisins, apples, cinnamon, and something else I couldn't divine.

"Maybe we spoke too soon about her," Rachel whispered. "Or maybe the thing is to just let her cook."

We pattered into the kitchen. She looked up and said, "Hey! Just in time." She opened the oven door and removed a cookie sheet sizzling with golden pastries. "Raspberries and cream cheese! Mmmmm. And I also made us some yummy oatmeal." She shimmied the pastries onto a cooling rack and then spooned the oatmeal into four deep bowls.

"Holy crap. The child can cook," Rachel said.

I moved to help Baby and she said, "No, no, no! I've got it!" She moved around the kitchen as if she knew exactly what she was doing. Barbara, Rachel, and I were mildly stunned. I looked at the table. It had already been set. A single rose in a crystal bud vase was nestled beside each of our napkins. "I'm sorry. I used frozen puff pastry. But I'm on vacation," she said, setting the bowls on the table and serving the pastries on individual dessert plates that were rimmed in gold. Lenox, if I had to guess.

"Nobody in their right mind makes it fresh," I murmured, taking in the luscious scents and the lovely place settings.

We took our seats and I gazed down at the rosy, steaming oatmeal with submerged bits of all sorts of goodness—apples, walnuts, raisins, brown sugar, cinnamon. "Wow," I said. "This smells delicious."

"It sure does," Barbara said. "And I'm famished."

"Go on. Eat," Baby said as she set the coffee carafe and a bowl of brown sugar on the table. The OJ had already been poured. "Anybody need anything else?"

"Nope. We're good," Barbara said and pulled out the chair next to her, indicating it was time for Baby to sit down and enjoy breakfast with us.

"To the chef!" I said, raising my spoon.

"Hear, hear!" the girls rang out all round. And we dug in.

"Baby, I'm mad at you," Rachel said, her mouth full of pastry.

"Why?" Baby batted her eyes as if she were girding herself for another onslaught from Rachel.

"You've been holding out on us. Damn! You can cook, honey."

"This is the best oatmeal I've ever eaten. It's real. None of that out-of-the-packet instant stuff," Barbara said right before she shoveled in another big mouthful.

"It really is delicious," I said. "What is in with the berries? A liquor..."

"Chambord," Baby said.

"Well, it's just perfect," I said, and Baby beamed. I gobbled down three or four good spoonfuls, relishing every single bite, and suddenly I was struck. I didn't even have time to speak or warn anyone or run to the bathroom. I simply slewed around in my chair and threw up on the floor.

"Oh, Madison...," Barbara began.

Baby shrieked. Rachel stopped eating, her spoon in mid air.

"I am *so* sorry," I said, scrubbing at my face and bending over to quell the suds in my stomach. "I don't know what..."

"What in the name of God?" Rachel slid back her

chair and wet a hand towel with cool water. She held it to my face.

Baby began to whimper. "I'm so, so sorry! Oh my God. Is it the food?"

"No, Baby. It's not the food," Barbara said softly, and I clutched my stomach, afraid I was going to heave again.

Baby burst into tears.

"No, Baby. It's not you. I-I-I just don't feel good," I said stupidly.

"Let's get you into bed," Rachel said. "Baby, get her some water. Just take it upstairs. She'll be OK. I'll clean up down here."

With Barbara's help, I made it down the hall and to the bathroom where I proceeded to vomit again. After the room stopped spinning, Baby and Barbara helped me upstairs where I spent most of the day shuttling between my room and the bathroom, throwing up. I was so woozy, hugged the wall coming and going. In between bathroom visits, I stayed in bed rereading *Jude the Obscure*, which I'd found wedged between the mattress and the wall.

"If the stomach flu doesn't get you, Jude certainly will," Barbara said, coming in with a cold cloth for my head. "God, if there is a more depressing book on the planet, I don't know what it would be."

I scooched up to a sitting position and my head spun. Barbara placed the cloth on my forehead.

"Is Baby OK?" I asked.

"Yeah, but she's still blaming herself even though we keep telling her it's not her fault that you picked up a bug."

"I'll have to apologize tomorrow." I closed my eyes, hoping to thwart another stomach upheaval.

"For what? It's not your fault you got sick."

"I just feel bad, Babs. She actually made a really good breakfast and I ruined it."

"I wouldn't worry about it. Good cook or not, she's just a self-involved little rich girl."

"I don't agree. I know she's annoying, but I think she's got more going on upstairs than we've given her credit for. Maybe Teddy didn't make a mistake after all."

"Damn, you really are sick. You must have brain fever."

I didn't respond. She paced the room, silent, and I closed my eyes, hoping to stanch the nausea by staying still. "You ought to go home and let Mac look you over," Barbara said finally. "You don't look good. We can get hold of that ferry fella and have him fetch you before he heads to New York."

Despite the fact that the last thing my stomach, in its current condition, could tolerate was a boat ride, I actually longed to go home, to climb into my own fresh lavender-smelling sheets and simply sleep, listening to Mac's voice as I drifted off. We read together most nights; he was currently reading me the poems of T. S. Eliot. I did not think I liked Eliot, but the night before I had left he read me "The Hollow Men," and I had wept aloud.

I could not have said why the poem affected me so; it simply seemed unutterably sad to me. Mac had held me close to him all night and, from time to time, I would wake up and breathe in his scent—sweat and soap and the Burberry cologne he favored—and the sadness engendered by the poem ebbed each time.

"No, I'll be OK," I said to Barbara. Beyond the issue with the boat ride, I wanted to make the rest of our time out here count for Rachel. "I'll be good as new by morning. I promise."

I felt a tremendous urge to confide in Barbara, to unburden myself, to tell her that our dearest friend on the planet was dying. Maybe that's why I was so sick. Keeping the secret was poisoning me. But I had given Rachel my word. And I would not go back on it. I squeezed Barbara's hand. "I think I'm already feeling better," I lied.

*   *   *

I do not know what the girls did Wednesday evening. Around six p.m. Barbara gave me a sleeping pill, which I gladly accepted, and I slept straight through to morning. When I awoke I felt human again. The sun streamed through the windows and French door. I rolled over and looked at the bedside clock. Nine a.m. I could not remember the last time I'd slept that late. I got out of bed, pulled on my bathing suit, threw a cover-up over it, and ventured downstairs. I heard the girls chattering on the front porch. After I got my coffee, I went out and joined them. Barbara and Rachel, that is. Baby was not in attendance.

"How are you feeling?" Barbara asked.

"Loads better," I said. I sipped my coffee and stared at the endless morning blue.

"Rachel was just telling me about the time she and Oliver did it in the front seat of his Jaguar."

"Stick shift?" I asked.

"Oh, yeah," Rachel said.

We were laughing about that, and I was trying to erase images of the two of them getting hot and heavy amid the leather and glass and instrument panel, when Baby burst out of the house, said, "Hello, y'all," and started off down the beach hugging a bulging grocery sack so close I thought that surely it must contain precious cargo. "You feeling better?" she asked.

"Much. Sorry I ruined your wonderful breakfast."

She flashed a brilliant smile and then kept going. "You didn't ruin anything. So glad you're better." Her words trailed behind her like wisps of smoke.

"What's in the sack?" I called after her.

"Sandwiches."

"Who are you feeding?" Rachel asked.

"Nobody," she said, picking up speed.

"Well ain't she Little Miss Tom Sawyer," Barbara said.

"What in the world? It's as if she doesn't want anything to do with us. What did y'all do to her?" I asked.

Barbara immediately looked guilty but Rachel gave away nothing.

"Barbara?"

"We just sort of roughed her up a little bit about Teddy last night."

"Oh, come on back, Baby. For God's sake." Rachel sighed and rolled her eyes. "We're sorry we acted like numbskulls last night. It was the wine. Besides, Teddy will kill us if he thinks we ran you off."

Baby turned around and faced us, but she kept going, walking backward. "I'm busy. I'll see you later."

"Where are you going?" Rachel stood and planted her hands on her hips, and I thought for a moment she might run down the beach and tackle our problem child.

Baby stopped and turned. She seemed to consider her answer for a couple of seconds, and then said, "Actually, it's none of your business."

Rachel gasped and I started laughing. Baby headed off again, and soon she and her bag of sandwiches were a memory.

"At this rate we'll have to go over to the mainland and get more food," Barbara groused.

"Oh, she'll bring it back," I said. "She can't possibly eat all that. Let her be. She's just being...a baby."

"Spoiled brat is more like it," Rachel said.

I looked at my dying friend. She appeared absolutely fearless, prompting me to wonder if she was cycling through Kübler-Ross's stages of grief or if a sense of one's mortality infused a soul with clarity, wrongheaded or otherwise. I took a deep breath. Frankly, at that moment, I felt as though it was all too much to think about. "It's OK. I suspect she'll be back in a couple of hours. But y'all must have surely pissed her off."

As it turned out, I was wrong. Baby did not return until late evening, and she did not bring back the food. To make matters more puzzling, she was gone when everyone got up the next morning.

"Hallelujah. The little nut job is MIA," Rachel said, stretching and stifling a yawn. "Who's for pancakes?" We'd gathered in the kitchen for morning coffee. It had become a ritual.

"Not me," I said. The nausea was threatening to creep back, and I was well aware that I was tottering slightly. "I think I need some warm milk. Do we have any milk?"

Rachel looked at me sharply, her brow knitted with concern. "Really?"

"Really."

"Sit down," Barbara said. "I'll make you some. How about I make it like I did for my kids when they were little—with a little sugar and a dash of vanilla?"

"Sounds great," I murmured, sliding into a kitchen chair.

Rachel pulled a carton of eggs out of the refrigerator, set them on the counter, and then handed Barbara a gallon of milk. "You don't have any kids still at home, do you?" she asked.

"Just one. Steven. But he heads to Vandy at the end of the month. I'm well on my way to being an empty nester."

"God," Rachel said, catching her breath, "they grow up so quickly, don't they?"

Barbara, oblivious, said, "I'm scared witless about it. I mean, Steven is hardly home anymore anyway with all his running around. But he sleeps at home. I like having another person in the house."

"And I guess Hugh doesn't count," I said, laughing.

"No, no he does not," she said, pouring a stream of cold milk into the pan.

I looked at Rachel, tried to catch her eye to let her know I was with her, that I loved her, but she was deep into her tough-as-nails persona. The only thing that might have indicated what she had really meant by the no-kids-at-home comment was the fierceness with which she scrambled those eggs.

The three of us sat on the front porch in the strengthening sunlight and sea breeze, me sipping sweet warm milk and Rachel and Barbara eating eggs and sliced tomatoes. We chatted about diets and face-lifts and how, for the most part, we were determined to eschew both. Of course, Barbara had already lost a ton of weight, so an empty promise about avoiding diets was easy for her to make.

I looked at the ocean—it was nearly translucent, like Caribbean water—and had almost started to say, "I wish we'd gone someplace else, as pretty as it is here, because Baby is just about the end of me. I'm worried sick about her," when we spied her heading toward us with nothing but her bikini bottoms on.

"Here we go," Barbara said under her breath.

Baby had barely placed one foot on the steps when Rachel said, "Let me guess. Tan lines."

"Baby, where have you been?" I asked.

"Oh, just here and there," she said, smiling. "There's a lovely spot in the middle of the island. I'll take y'all there if you'd like," and then she drifted into the house as if she were a feather floating in a breeze.

"I swear to God," Rachel said after she was out of earshot, "if this place wasn't hers, I'd call up Teddy and tell him to come get her."

"And I'd pack her bags," Barbara said.

"Well, we've only got a week to go," I said, standing. I ambled to the far side of the porch and gazed at the sun-dappled Atlantic. "Let's enjoy ourselves, no matter what. OK?"

I felt the urgency of my words so intently that I kept my back to the girls so they would not see the tears that threatened to well and fall.

CHAPTER

6

The rest of that day and the next were unremark-
able. The weather remained warm and still and
so quiet that the July flies in the trees were loud as a
choir. But odd things kept happening... irritations
and accidents that put Barbara, Rachel, and me on
edge.

Baby mainly steered clear of us; over the next
three days her manic behavior seemed to have turned
into low, simmering hostility. Over lunch she told
Rachel that she should "lose the Yankee accent," and
when Barbara said during a Sunday-afternoon ocean
dip that she wondered if men needed sex more than
women or if some were simply genetically coded to
cheat, Baby said, "Men cheat on women who deserve
it."

In lieu of slapping her, I slapped the water—it's

lucky she wasn't within arm's reach or I might have
grabbed her by the hair and yanked hard.

"Baby, that's the most asinine thing to come out of
your mouth yet," I snapped.

"Oh yeah?" she said. "Look who's talking." And
then she splashed out of the flaccid surf and stomped
up to the house, muttering to herself the entire way.

"What exactly did y'all say to her when I was laid
up in bed?" I asked.

"Rachel told her that Teddy had a thing for blondes
with money, that love didn't have anything to do with
it."

"You told her what! Why, Rachel, that's just plain
mean."

"No," Rachel said, her face hardening. "It's the
truth. Life is too short not to know the truth."

I was speechless. Rachel wasn't a cruel person, but
what she'd said to Baby was cruel. No wonder Baby
was making herself scarce. And by the stubborn ex-
pressions on Barbara's and Rachel's faces, I knew it
would be up to me to try to make things right.

We spent another couple of hours at the beach and
went back up to the house. From the looks of the
kitchen—a half-eaten sandwich and a mug of beer
that had barely been sipped—it was clear that Baby
had taken off in a hurry, probably when she heard us
coming.

So that evening, over a dinner of gazpacho, chilled

shrimp, and green salad, I said, "Listen, I know Baby tries our patience. But we're not mean people. So tomorrow, no matter if it's stormy or sunny, we're going to walk over to the bay side and see if we can find where Baby keeps escaping to, and what she does there. And we're going to be nice about it."

"If she's having an affair," Barbara said, "Teddy deserves to know, even if we're mad at him."

"Damn straight," Rachel said.

"OK, fine," I said. This was not going the way I wanted it to. "But we have no evidence of any affair."

"Yeah, right," Rachel grumbled before pouring more wine.

*   *   *

Monday morning after breakfast, we put our plan into effect. Or at least we tried. I sat on the hammock and grabbed my sneakers, which I'd left there overnight. I slipped them on and stood up. The pain was instant and fierce. I cried out, but still the bee trapped in my right shoe buzzed ferociously while it stung me. I kicked off the sneaker, yowling, and the poor bee flew away, wobbly, as though it were punch-drunk. With pain searing through my foot, I examined the shoe from heel to toe, fearing that an entire colony had set up shop in there.

"A bee. It stung me," I said to Barbara and Rachel,

who were rushing out of the house in response to my yelping.

In no time, my foot swelled up to the size of a small watermelon.

"How in the hell did a bee get into your sneakers?" Rachel asked.

"I don't know."

I waved my two friends off and hobbled into the house. It hurt, surprisingly badly. I made a paste of aspirin and seawater that Barbara fetched for me—a poultice, of sorts. The pain, but not the swelling, subsided just a hair.

Rachel, scowling with worry, inspected my foot. "It looks like you've been snakebit."

"If it were a snakebite, I'd already be dead. Besides, I saw it. It was definitely a bee."

"It makes no sense. None at all," Rachel said, glowering.

"I brought some Benadryl with me," Barbara said. "Stay here. I'll go get it."

After an hour's delay, determined not to let something as minor as a beesting spoil our reconnaissance expedition, I said from my hammock perch, "OK, I think I'm ready."

Barbara looked up over her interior design magazine and said, "You're not going anywhere."

"That's right. Today we're taking it easy. Gin and tonics at lunch. I'm cooking. A nap in the afternoon.

Tomorrow, we'll see. But you, Mrs. McCauley, are going to take it easy." Rachel was a very effective drill sergeant.

By the time I fell into bed that night, my foot was sore but noticeably better. As I dozed off, faint optimism soothed me. No more stomach flu, I thought. No more vomiting. No more insect stings. No more nothing but a good time. Surely we could make that happen.

And then, in the middle of the night, during a pretty decent dream in which Mac and I were planting a seaside garden composed solely of giant ruby flowers, my bed collapsed. Stunned, I spilled onto the floor, cracking my chin hard. Barbara and Rachel came running in, their hair and pajamas and Rachel's eye mask all asunder.

"What in blazes happened?" Rachel asked.

"Looks like the leg plumb broke off," Barbara said, bending down and retrieving it. "Baby!" she yelled.

"No use," Rachel said, helping me to my feet. "She's not here. You all right?"

"Yeah, I think so," I said, confused because sleep still swaddled me, yet a part of my brain was wildly awake.

Barbara studied the leg, frowning. "It's just an old bed. And an old leg. It wobbled loose. See?" She showed us the end that fit into the post. "It needs to be replaced. That's all."

"Well, Maddy," Rachel said, studying the leg, "you

sure are having more than your fair share of bad luck."

"Where am I going to sleep?" I wondered aloud, looking at the lopsided bed.

"With Baby? She's never there anyway." Barbara started laughing.

"No. Bricks!" Rachel snapped her fingers. There's a pile out by the Third Eye. We'll just stack them up and make a leg."

That's how the three of us found ourselves outside, in the dark, in our pajamas, sifting through a spider-filled pile of bricks on a nearly deserted island in a dark sea. Rachel was in charge, tossing aside two for every one we kept. Barbara and I both had just about all we could carry when Babs whispered, "Ho-ly shi-iit." She pointed toward the trees.

"What?" Rachel asked, bent over, rear in the air. We both followed the line of Barbara's finger and spied, in the cloud-shadowed moonlight, two amber eyes staring at us from the cover of the hammock jungle. Whatever animal they belonged to let out a low, slow growl.

We screamed, dropped the bricks, and ran. We stumbled up the steps and nearly flew through the door, which Rachel locked and then flung herself against, as if the animal sought to burst in.

"Oh my God," Barbara said, leaning over, catching her breath, "that was a freaking bobcat!"

"It sure as hell was," I said. I had never seen a bob-cat, but it seemed logical.

"Jesus." Rachel jiggled the door handle, made sure she had securely locked it. "Is Baby safe? Out there wandering around like a yard dog?"

Barbara started laughing. She flopped onto the couch and held her sides. "Oh God, oh God, oh God!"

Rachel and I exchanged bewildered glances.

"What...if...," Barbara choked out between guf-faws, "Baby got...eaten by a...bobcat!"

I sank down next to her, suddenly convulsed. "Why, Teddy would be beside himself."

"Yeah, poor tail-chasing Teddy," Rachel choked, doubling over. "Here lies the third Mrs. Teddy Pat-terson, mauled to death by a bobcat while she wan-dered a desert island naked as a jaybird, in search of younger tail."

We all guffawed and finally I said, trying to catch my breath, "It's really not funny."

"Oh, she's all right. She's holed up somewhere all safe and sound. Our Baby isn't a roughing-it type of girl," Barbara said.

"You're right." I nodded. I felt the laughter die and remembered the intensity of the bobcat's eyes. So beautiful. So scary. As the adrenaline rush ebbed, a leaden fatigue took its place.

"So, I guess it's the couch for me."

"Nope," Rachel said, pointing at the bookcase. "I don't know why I didn't think of books in the first place."

"Great idea! We'll get you back in the bed come hell or high water," Barbara said, tousling my hair.

And that's what we did. We made a fourth leg out of books. I shimmied in *Jude the Obscure* between *The Birds of South Carolina* and a children's book about a farting dog.

"This must be Baby's," Rachel said when she handed it to me.

With the bed level and secure, we admitted that we'd had enough excitement for one night. Barbara and Rachel went back to their rooms. I snuggled between my sheets, and when I closed my eyes and dozed off, my dreams were filled with wild, yellow-eyed animals gazing at blue water under purple, moonlit skies.

*   *   *

I was soundly asleep, at peace with my dreams, when, deep into the night, a sharp scream pierced my consciousness. In my groggy state, at first I thought all the animals must be bounding through the jungle, a Tiger Island stampede, but as the layers of sleep evaporated, I realized that what I was hearing was the sound of feet hitting the floor. I switched on my bedside light, tried to get my bearings, and hobbled out of bed and into the hall.

Barbara rushed out of her room, screaming, arms flailing, and slammed her door.

Rachel burst from her room, crying, "What the hell now!"

Barbara pointed to her bedroom with one hand and kept her face covered with the other.

"It's horrible," she cried. "They're attacking me!"

"Nobody is attacking anybody," Rachel said as she and I ran to Barbara's room and cracked open the door.

"Dear God!" I could barely believe my eyes. The window screen was gone. A huge swarm of insects was pouring into the room and circling her bed in a black maelstrom. Some of the bugs were enormous. We shut the door and pulled Barbara downstairs and into the kitchen, where we examined the damage.

She had suffered a couple of savage bites on her face and many small ones all over. She looked as if she had smallpox, chicken pox, measles, and leprosy. I sat her down at the kitchen table and applied ice-filled washcloths to the bites. Rachel ventured back upstairs to see if the screen was on the porch. She returned moments later and retrieved the flashlight from the pantry.

"It's in the fucking yard," she said. "How did it get in the fucking yard?" She headed for the front door.

"Watch out for the bobcat!" I yelled, and then tried to hide how freaked out I was by plastering a silly grin on my face, because Barbara was badly shaken. The last thing she needed was for me to lose it.

"Here," I said, pouring her a glass of wine. "Drink this. Keep the ice on your face. I'll be right back."

I ran upstairs to retrieve the calamine lotion I'd brought with me at Mac's insistence, but first I checked Baby's room. She was gone and the bed hadn't been slept in.

Something surely isn't right here, I thought as I returned with the calamine. "This stuff isn't going to make you any prettier," I said, "but it'll stop the itching."

Barbara knocked back a healthy slug of wine. "I swallowed one," she sobbed. "It was a big one. I think it was a June bug."

Rachel returned, carrying the screen. "I can't imagine how it ended up out there."

"Baby's bed hasn't been slept in," I said, my concern deepening. Seemed like trouble was befalling us all at once.

"Do you think she's fucking with us?" Barbara asked, still trembling.

"I don't," I said slowly as I smoothed the calamine over Barbara's bites. "Of course not. She's not a bee whisperer or a bobcat conjurer."

"I don't like this at all," Rachel snapped.

"In the meantime, what do we do?" Barbara gingerly touched her swelling face.

"Well, I've shut the window in your room," Rachel said. "So I'm going to go in search of bug spray. I think I saw some in the vanity in my bathroom. I'll crack open the door and shoot the spray in, fogging the place. By morning they should all be dead."

"Sounds like a plan," I said. "And Barbara, just bunk with me tonight. Me with my swollen foot and you with your swollen face."

Barbara nodded, laughing and crying at the same time.

"You two go on to bed, you limping, swollen fools. I'll take care of this mess," Rachel said.

"You sure, Rach?" I asked.

"Shhh, not another word."

I helped Barbara up the stairs and into my bed. The wine worked wonders. She fell asleep in no time. I lay awake, listening to Rachel cuss ("Die, you damned bastards!") and to the hiss of the bug spray can she emptied into Barbara's room. I heard her wash up in the bathroom and then patter into her bedroom.

When I was sure all the crying and cursing and spraying had ended for the night, I drifted back to sleep. And this time I did not dream.

*   *   *

The next morning, as the three of us sat around the kitchen table drinking coffee, eating stale pound cake topped with thawed frozen blueberries, and watching Barbara slather on more calamine, Baby waltzed down the stairs and into the kitchen. She must have slipped in sometime after we'd finally gone to bed for the last time.

She looked at Barbara and then ambled over to the fridge, where she surveyed its contents. I noticed her legs were scratched up to her knees.

"What happened to you?" she asked.

"Bugs," Barbara said between swollen lips.

"A bee in my shoe," I said.

"Hmmm." She retrieved the milk and proceeded to pour herself a huge bowl of cereal. "Teddy and I noticed they were bad this season. But, you know, if you keep the doors and windows shut and turn on the overhead fan…"

"Yeah," Rachel said, shooting her a long, don't-tread-on-me look. "You'd think that would do it, wouldn't you?"

"It's just common sense." Baby leaned against the counter and began to eat.

Rachel's dark eyes flashed. Something, I knew, was about to break, and my days of running interference were over.

"You know what common sense is, Baby?"

"Of course I do."

"Really? And we're supposed to accept—as if we're a bunch of stooges—that a bee finds its way into Madison's shoe all by itself? And somehow a bed leg is so loose that it tumbles over? And in the middle of the night, Barbara's screen falls out of its own volition? Really?"

"I don't know what you're talking about." Baby set her bowl on the counter and started to walk out. Rachel stood, blocking her path.

"Oh, I think you know exactly what I'm talking about!"

Barbara and I exchanged glances. I couldn't believe that Rachel was actually accusing Baby of these various mishaps. "Now, Rachel, you can't possibly believe that Baby put a bee in my shoe."

"The hell I can't!"

Baby crossed her arms. She lifted her face and tried to look Rachel in the eye, but she was no match.

"What do you want, Rachel?"

"I want the truth."

Baby stamped her foot. "I don't know what you're talking about. Leave me alone!"

"Tell us the truth, Baby, or I'm going to tell Teddy about your fling with that handsome Gullah man."

Baby sneered. "My affair! Go ahead. He won't believe you because there *is no affair*."

"When I get done, little girl, I'll have him convinced you're fucking everything on this island. And you know I can do it. You may be his latest piece of tail, but I've known that man for over twenty years. Don't even tempt me."

Barbara pushed her chair back and said in her cool schoolteacher's voice, "Baby, we don't care what you did. That's over. Except we could have been hurt really badly."

I shot Barbara a horrified glare. "Oh come on," I said, but she ignored me.

"I mean, look at me, Baby. I look like I have small-pox. Plus, that damned bobcat could have jumped through the window and mauled us all. Where on earth did you get him?"

"Ladies," I said, "this is nuts."

"Bobcat?" Baby looked truly confused.

"Yes, Baby, bobcat," Rachel said. "How did you manage to stage that?"

Baby grabbed her hair, the way a child does before a full-throttle tantrum. "I don't know about any stupid bobcat!"

"But you do know about the bee and the bed and the bugs. Don't you, Baby?" Barbara's voice was a perfect mix of kindness and admonition. "You need to tell us so that we can get past this and move on."

Barbara was really good. Rachel was an attack dog, but Barbara was the soft feather with a poison-tipped quill.

"Baby?" Barbara said, all soft and motherly. I

couldn't look at her because her voice was soothing but her face was a calamine- and bite-pocked mess.

"What, what, what?" Baby yelled, and then she burst into tears.

Barbara stood, reached out, and hugged her.

"Now, now," she crooned.

Baby pulled away.

"I didn't do anything wrong! Have I been really hurt and pissed after you two ganged up on me? Yes! But I would never hurt anybody! For your information, I'm a pacifist. That's why I learned Arabic!" She was hiccupping through her tears.

"What does speaking Arabic have to do with being a pacifist?" I asked. Now I was the one who was profoundly confused.

"Because," Baby said as if speaking to a moron, "if someone has declared a holy war on you, perhaps the best thing to do is learn their language so you can talk to them! You think I'm stupid but I'm not," she screamed. "And Teddy loves me for my brains. Not for my money. He's got his own money. I will never be Melinda Patterson, God rest her soul. I'm just me, Baby, and I love Teddy with all my heart."

Rachel scrubbed her face with her palms and said, "OK. So you didn't do any of these shenanigans?"

"No!"

"The wind was blowing hard last night. It just blew the screen out, caught it like a sail," I said.

"That bed leg has been loose for a while. I told Teddy to fix it, but I guess he forgot. I'm sorry, Maddy. That must have been quite a fright."

"And the bee was just wrong place, wrong time," Barbara murmured.

"Shit," Rachel said, recognizing defeat.

"OK, Baby," Barbara said. "We all could have handled things differently. And we're all going to say we're sorry. I'll start. I'm sorry. Rachel?"

Rachel glared at Barbara. Clearly Rachel thought Barbara had lost her mind, even though it was clear that Baby had not been the culprit, that indeed there had been no culprit. Barbara mouthed, "Do it!"

She looked away and shook her head.

"We all make mistakes," I said, "and it looks like this one was a doozy. I'm sorry, Baby."

"Yeah," Rachel said, putting one arm behind her back and crossing her index and bird fingers, "me too."

Barbara shot her a brief smile and nodded her thanks. "Do you forgive us? Can we just move on?"

Baby sniffled. "Yeah. Of course."

"Here," Barbara said, handing Baby a napkin. "Now wipe your nose and go get dressed. We're going to do something with our day."

Blowing her nose and still sniveling, Baby obliged.

Until we heard the bathroom water run, the three of us remained silent, cautious. But as soon as we heard the creak and whoosh of old pipes and the burping of the rusty water, we let loose.

"Damn it," Rachel said. "I feel like a shit heel. How did you do that, Barbara? Make it all right after we just about accused her of attempted murder?"

"That," I said, nodding at Barbara, "is twenty years of dealing with seventh-graders." I looked at her and beamed. "Good job!"

"Yeah, but in this case, we're the seventh-graders and she's the adult," Rachel said. "Since I was the one spearheading the accusers, I'll go clean up Barbara's room."

"You will do absolutely no such thing," I said.

"Absolutely not. I will clean up my own room myself."

Rachel's eyes settled on me and I read them right: Everything in her dwindling days mattered. I relented. "All right."

So we waited. Barbara poured herself a glass of wine. Rachel reached for the broom and dustpan that were tilted into the space between the fridge and counter and went upstairs. I popped open a bottle of fizzy water. It felt cool and soothing going down. Only a handful of minutes passed before we heard Baby's footsteps on the stairs. We stayed silent. She walked into the kitchen, her face freshly washed but still blotchy from the tears.

"Where's Rachel?" she asked.

"You just missed her."

"She's in my room, cleaning up the bug carnage."

"Oh," Baby said. "Well, I need to go help."

"Not sure that's a good idea," Barbara said, pressing the cool wineglass against her swollen face.

Baby turned on her heel and marched out of the kitchen, saying, "Nope. If I'd put that screen in right in the first place, it would have never blown out."

Barbara dropped her head into her hands. "Oh, God."

"What's wrong, Babs?"

"She just keeps proving us wrong. I wish we'd been right. It would feel so much better than the guilt."

I started laughing. "Oh, I'm sure she'll do something that outrages us. Probably before nightfall. And then the universe will be back in balance."

Barbara smiled and reached for my hand. "*Merci beaucoup, cher ami.* I'd kiss you except I'm hideous." She smoothed back her hair. "I'm going to take a shower, get this junk off my face, and wash my hair. And then, Madison McCauley"—she looked determined, set jaw and all—"we're rebooting this vacation."

*   *   *

While Baby and Rachel were busy setting Barbara's room in order, including by changing the Raid-soaked sheets, Barbara and I sat on the front porch, mulling over our options for the day, which were admittedly limited. The idea of exploring the other side of the island and introducing ourselves to Earl's family had caught our imaginations, but there was a bobcat on the loose.

"With our track record, he'd probably eat every single one of us," I said.

"Except for Baby," Barbara said. "He'd probably curl up in her lap."

"We've got her spic-'n'-span clean, y'all. Not a bug in sight!" Baby trilled, bounding onto the porch, Coca-Cola in hand.

She flopped into a rocking chair and said, "Ah-hhh."

"Hallelujah!" Barbara said.

"Amen," Rachel said, letting the screen door bang behind her.

"Now, listen," Baby said, wiping sweat off the cån, "I want to take y'all to where I go. My pretty spot in the woods."

"Bobcat," Rachel said.

"Was it really a bobcat?" Baby asked.

"Its eyes glowed in the moonlight and the fucker growled." Rachel swirled her iced coffee.

"Well." Baby smacked her lips. "Whatever it was, it won't be out in the middle of the day."

"Are you sure?" Barbara asked.

"Absolutely."

Then, as if bobcats were no big deal and Baby were trustworthy, Barbara said, "Y'all, let's do it! I mean, why the hell not?"

Rachel and I exchanged glances and then looked at Barbara and Baby, who appeared completely at ease with the idea. I threw up my hands. "All right. But if I get mauled, my remains will never forgive you."

*   *   *

We walked in a ragged line until we reached the thick hammock and were forced to go single file with Baby in the lead.

"Are you sure we're not going to get snakebit, Baby?" I asked.

"Just follow the path."

"What path?" Rachel asked.

"The one we're on."

We'd trudged through the jungle no longer than fifteen or twenty minutes before it opened into a vast sea of pluff mud. A stickier, smellier, more unpleasant substance would be hard to find on this earth, but marsh grass, crabs, and oysters love the stuff. You have to be careful walking in it, though, because you could get sucked down, just as if you were in a bed of wet concrete. A ribbon of sand and grass bisected the pluff mud, and on the other side a lovely glade opened, gleaming like an emerald.

"Wow! You're right, Baby. A pretty spot for sure!" I said.

The glade, complete with wildflowers and butter-flies, was ringed with palmettos and old, moss-draped, stately oaks. The morning sun shone through the mottled clouds, sending down shafts of what looked like pure gold.

"We used to call those holy miracle rays," Rachel said, surveying the sky, the jungle canopy, the glade.

"Yep. Just like those Jesus pictures in Sunday school," Barbara said, her eyes following the slant of sunbeams.

Baby ran ahead of us and we followed, crossing the grass-and-sand bridge to the other side. Once in the glade, Baby said, "See why I love it! See how sweet it is? Sometimes I just need a break from the ocean."

"It really is gorgeous," Rachel said, "and quiet."

"So you sleep out here?" I asked.

"No, no, not really." And then she did a cartwheel, which was, I realized, not so much a bid for attention as an evasive move.

"We should have a picnic here," Barbara said, studying a blooming cloud bank in the distance.

"Yes!" Baby said, and before the *s* was dry on her tongue, we heard a violent rustling in the under-growth, and Barbara screamed, "Bobcat!"

We shrieked and ran into each other as we tried to flee, and a herd of squealing, snorting feral hogs burst out of the jungle and charged us. I moved left when I should have moved right. One fleeing hog's tusk got me along my shin. The pain was immediate. I looked down and saw a long, shallow, bleeding gash. For some reason, perhaps it was my subconscious's way to ignore the pain, I thought only, *Damn it—that's going to scar.*

"Son of a bitch!" Rachel yelled, spinning around to Baby.

"Oh, Maddy, I didn't know! Really, I didn't!" Baby pleaded. "I mean, I knew the Gullahs kept pigs, but they were fenced in. They've always been fenced in. I've never seen these wild ones. Never ever!"

"Kinda hard to miss them," Rachel said, giving Baby another of her long, heavy-lidded stares.

"Oh goodness!" Barbara said, and I threw up. Again. And my knees wobbled as if Jell-O had replaced bone. I would have fallen if Rachel hadn't caught me and lowered me to the grass.

"I think you need a doctor for that," she said, whipping her turquoise kerchief from around her neck and stanching the bleeding. "Damn, I wish I could get hold of Hugh, or somebody who knows something about pigs..."

"I didn't know Hugh knew anything about pigs," Baby said in all seriousness.

Despite my pain and gut hurt and bleeding, I found Baby's statement hilarious. Through laughter and dry heaves, I sputtered, "God, no, I don't need Hugh! It was just a damned pig. Not even a feral one, either, if they belong to the Gullahs. There must be a fence..."

"Hmmm, you'd think so," Barbara said, and then she went over to where the pigs had burst out, to the high grass that bordered the underbrush. She knelt and examined a torn-up plot of earth. "Well, there was a fence, but it's broken down. See?" She retrieved an old, rotted fence stake. "The pieces of it are all over the place." She tossed it on the ground and walked back over to us. "You know, Maddy, I agree with Rachel. All this dizziness and throwing up...something isn't right."

"I swear I didn't sic the pigs on her," Baby said, reaching out for Barbara, her protector. "I had no idea there were crazed pigs running around out here."

"I know what's not right," Rachel said, smiling. "It ain't pigs and it ain't the stomach flu and it ain't you, Baby."

"Then what is it?" Baby's eyes were huge, as if she feared the answer.

"It's Mac."

We looked at Rachel in disbelief. Baby, who appeared profoundly confused, in fact nearly cross-eyed, cried, "What!"

"It's called pregnant. Plain as the nose on your face, you're pregnant, Maddy."

"But I... but we've never...," I started.

"You still do it, don't you?" Rachel was laser-locked on me. There was no escape.

"Well, of course! But in all these years..."

"Listen, if I don't know pregnant when I see it, nobody does." Rachel pushed my hair off my face. "Don't forget, I've got five. Congratulations, Maddy. We're delighted for you!"

"Now that you mention it," Barbara said—a wide smile dispelling the look of terror that had been on her face ever since she yelled "Bobcat!"—"it makes perfect sense!"

I offered no more bewildered protests, but inside my heart sang. *Could it be true? Could it finally, finally be true? After all this time...*

"A baby!" Baby exclaimed, bouncing on her toes, clapping.

I looked at their three beaming faces and decided I simply would not think about the possibility that I was actually carrying a child until I got home. Nothing was going to seem real until then anyway. Whenever anyone mentioned it, I decided, I would simply hold up my hand and silence her. Those were the last thoughts I had before everything went black.

*   *   *

When I came to, the first thing I saw was a whirring fan and then a nut-brown face, eyes the same shade as Barbara's, but it wasn't Barbara.

"There you are." She applied a cool compress to my forehead. "Just too much excitement for a pregnant lady on a hot, hot day." She had a lovely lilting accent.

For a moment I thought I was dreaming. Or dead. But then there they all were, a circle of concerned faces hovering over me: Rachel, Barbara, Baby, this woman, and Earl.

"What happened?" I mumbled, trying to sit up, but the woman pushed me gently back down.

"You passed out," Rachel said.

"And we couldn't wake you," Barbara said.

"So I ran and got Earl," Baby piped up. "He carried you here to Mama Bonaparte's house."

Mama Bonaparte. The name was strange yet familiar, but before I could begin to place it or form a coherent thought she said, "And you are my little Mac's wife. I haven't seen him in so, so long. You tell that child that Mama B misses him and he needs to come see us."

"Oh, my," I said, the fog lifting. "Mac has told me about you, how during his summers out here, you practically raised him."

"I did raise him," she said, pride lighting her voice. "And now look." She reached over and hugged Earl.

"My grandson and his wife lose their first baby—nothing can heal that sadness—but here you come, delivered to me in the arms of my grandson, and you're bearing my Mac's child. Such a mysterious world," she whispered.

Earl hugged his grandmother, and Baby put her arms around them both. The weight of the loss clouded Earl's eyes. I wanted to get up and hug him too, but in my condition that wasn't going to happen. "It's going to be OK." Baby said it three times, like an incantation, a hopeful prayer.

"How do you all know each other?" Barbara asked.

Baby relaxed her grip on Earl but didn't let go. Mama Bonaparte tested my skin with the back of her hand, placing it on my forehead, my cheek, and finally my throat.

"It's something Mac and I have in common," Baby said. "I wanted to talk to him about it when we visited you in Charleston, but, I dunno. I got shy or something. Earl, how long have I known you and Sharelle?"

Earl shook his head. "Baby, it's got to be, I don't know . . . since we could all walk?"

"I delivered you, child," Mama Bonaparte said to Baby.

"Who's Sharelle?" I asked.

"My wife. We're in mourning," Earl said, stating the obvious. "Our baby . . . he didn't even get a chance to see this world." Earl covered his eyes with the back of his arm and, once more, Baby held him, whispering that it would all be OK.

"So this is where you've been disappearing?" Rachel asked. "You've been coming out here to help your friends?"

Baby nodded yes. Earl slumped down in a chair beside Mama Bonaparte.

"Well, why didn't you tell us?"

"Because," Baby said, "I didn't want to ruin your vacation. And Earl and Sharelle are *my* friends. And you know what? When something like this happens, the last thing you want in this whole world is a bunch of strangers fussing over you."

"Oh, Baby," Rachel said, "we accused you of all manner of crap. I am really sorry."

And this time every one of us, even Baby, knew she meant it.

"Sounds like you all had quite a time," Mama Bonaparte said, studying my face.

"You can say that again," Barbara said.

"We quit keeping pigs a couple of years ago. Didn't we, Earl?" Mama Bonaparte said. "The boys do a good job of thinning out the wild ones. Nothing like this has ever happened before, dear. I feel responsible."

"Please don't apologize," I said, and I wondered how Mac could stay away so long. Mama B, as I would learn everyone called her, was a strong and loving woman. "Maybe it was meant to be. I mean, here we are, meeting you and all."

"Perhaps." She stroked my hair and then said, "Baby, can you go fix Miss Maddy a cup of tea?"

"Blackberry?"

"Indeed. And y'all go help her." She began fussing with the dressing bandage someone—I supposed it was Mama B—had applied to my leg. As the girls and Earl shuffled out, she said, "We don't want this getting infected. No, ma'am."

"I can't thank you enough," I said, and for no reason at all, I burst into tears. "It must be the hormones. I mean, if I really am pregnant."

"Oh, you're pregnant, all right." She got up, walked over to a bureau, and came back with some sort of salve.

"How can you be so sure?" I asked through tears.

"Honey, I've tended to all the pregnant ladies who have ever come out here, including Mac's mama." She removed the bandage and inspected the wound. "I would have delivered your husband had his mama timed it right." She applied the cool salve to the gash and then taped fresh gauze into place. "Listen to me." She took my hands in hers and my tears slowed. "I need you to tell Mac something for me. I need you to tell him that we all know he didn't do it."

"Do what?"

"He never told you?"

"No. He's never talked about Tiger. And he wasn't happy when it was decided we'd come out here."

Mama B pursed her lips, stared into space, seemed to find her answer, gazed down at me, and said, "Somebody stole my son-in-law's boat. This was a long time ago. And James...well, James is a bit of a hothead and he immediately went off, accusing your Mac of being the thief. It wasn't true. We all knew it wasn't true. But the accusation cut Mac to the quick. He has his pride, as I'm sure you know."

Mac's pride. I did know. It was a quiet pride but as massive and immovable as a barrier reef. No, Mac wouldn't have forgiven such an accusation. Nor would he have told me about it.

"And once it was all settled," she went on, "once we figured out the boat hadn't been stolen at all but 'borrowed' for a joyride by some trash who came out here camping, Mac was already gone. False accusations have a way of tearing people to bits, you know. And we didn't have a clue how to find him. Besides, we thought he'd be back. We thought we could set things straight once he came home." It looked as if Mama B might be the one to cry next. "But he never did. And his family never rebuilt after Hugo. Land's just sitting there."

"What?" I felt as if the whole world were spinning under me. "You mean, we own land out here?"

"I think so. If your husband sold it, the buyers have made themselves scarce. As in nonexistent."

I lay there trying to wrap my mind around this—the second bombshell of the day—when the girls and Earl tumbled back into the room all atwitter. Baby was guffawing and Earl was laughing, and Barbara was exclaiming, "Wait till I tell my kids," and Rachel, above the din, shouted, "Madison, you are not going to believe this."

"What?" I couldn't think of one other thing that could surprise me on a day that was proving to be full of surprises.

"Look!" Rachel said.

The four of them parted, Mama B glanced over her shoulder, and I screamed.

"Don't be afraid," Earl said. "It's Bunny."

Rachel slapped her thigh. "Bunny! What a hysterical name for a … wildcat!"

"It wasn't a bobcat last night," Barbara said. "It was Bunny, Earl's pet ocelot."

I felt my forehead. Surely I was having fever-induced hallucinations. Before I could sit up and take stock of the situation, Bunny loped over to me and began licking my hand.

"She likes you!" Earl said.

"Such a good girl!" Mama B cooed. "Aren't you? Yes, you are. You keep loving on Miss Maddy and she'll be better in no time." And then Mama B proceeded to plant a kiss atop Bunny's tan-and-black-striped head. Bunny began purring like a huge, quiet engine. I was afraid and fascinated and possibly in love. She was beautiful.

"She goes to the bathroom in the toilet!" Baby crowed, setting my tea on the bedside table.

That had to be a lie. Crazy Baby.

"Why did she growl at us?" I asked Earl.

"From how Barbara and Rachel described it, with y'all throwing bricks, she was probably scared. But she's not supposed to be over on the beach anyway. I'm sorry. It's just, with Sharelle so upset and us losing the baby, we haven't been keeping up with anything. Bunny just decided to wander off for the night." He looked at Baby. "I guess she wasn't getting enough attention."

"No need to apologize," I said, gathering the nerve to pet Bunny down the length of her back. I could feel the satiny ripple of muscle all the way down. "We're really sorry about the baby, Earl."

"Yes, we are," Rachel said.

"Thank you. I appreciate that." He looked down at the floor. I could tell that he was trying to keep his composure.

The whole thing broke my heart. Nobody should lose a baby. This was a good family. Close-knit. Hardworking. Sweet-spirited. Why, Mama B's love for Mac was written all over her handsome face every time she spoke his name. I sat up and Mama B handed me my tea. As I took it from her I made a silent pledge to make sure the Bonaparte-McCauley fence got mended.

Mama B tested my forehead again. "You're going to be just fine," she said.

As if the prognosis were the permission she needed, Bunny jumped onto the bed, expertly avoiding my wound, and curled up by my feet.

"Looks like Bunny has found a new friend," Earl said.

"That's wonderful," I said, eyeing the beautiful cat. "I think."

Mama B turned and said, "Baby, I've got some greens on. Can you take Sharelle some? And don't forget the corn bread."

"Yes, ma'am," Baby said, no sass at all.

"And Earl, bring in that okra I picked this morning. I left it on the bench outside the shed. I'm going to fix our guests okra-and-tomato stew." Her smile deepened. I had a hunch this woman was quite a cook.

"I'm sorry, ladies," Earl said before he and Baby set out on their chores. "I'd love for you to meet Sharelle, but she just isn't up for visitors. Next time. You'll really like her."

"Does your wife need medical attention?" Rachel asked.

"Rachel here is a nurse," Barbara explained.

Earl shook his head. "No, no...Sharelle is, um..." He trailed off.

"She's just sad," Mama B finished his sentence for him. "Just real sad."

After Baby and Earl left, Mama B said, "All right, young lady, you feel like getting up?"

"I think so," I said. "And, I have to say, at the mention of okra and tomatoes, I realize that I'm starving."

"Good! Then let's all head to the kitchen. You girls can help. And you, Madison McCauley," she said, helping me to my feet, "can sit with your leg up. Like a queen bee."

And that's how we spent our afternoon. Gabbing as if we'd all known each other forever. Mama B spouted orders with gentle authority and chopped okra with hands scarred by hard work. Baby behaved like a totally different person. She was respectful and low-key, and never once took off her beach cover-up.

The question had been gnawing at me, so as we gathered around steaming bowls of white rice and okra and tomatoes cooked down with onions, garlic, salt, pepper, and some sort of hot spice I couldn't identify, I said, "I just have to know something. How do y'all deal with Miz Baby over here running around the island nearly naked?"

Earl looked up from his fragrant bowl of stew—he'd already dug into his—and began a slow, easy, rumbling laugh.

Mama B didn't look up. She simply broke some corn bread into her stew and said, "Around here we have none of that. Do we, Baby?"

"No, ma'am," Baby said. "Mothers..." She looked at us as though she were a prim schoolgirl and I thought, *If she starts up with this mothers thing I'm going to stab her.* Baby dabbed the corners of her mouth with her napkin, cleared her throat, and said in an angelic voice, "I never come to this side of the island without clothes on. It would be disrespectful. In fact, despite what you may think, I only occasionally skinny-dip. I am not," she added, her face haughty and precise, "a nudist."

Rachel shot her the Death Stare. In response, Baby gave us back a dazzling smile and poured herself more tea.

"You missed your calling, Baby," Barbara said.

"How's that?"

"You should have been an actress."

"That's what Teddy says!"

I shook my head. Actually, Baby was a stitch, and despite my reservations, I realized that I couldn't help but like her. I took a deep breath. My stomach was calm and I was ready for some delicious Mama B food. I ate and ate, and with each spoonful I felt the health and warmth seep back into my bones.

"Mmmmm," I said, closing my eyes, letting the

goodness of the food take hold, "this is absolutely delicious."

*   *   *

After the lunch dishes were washed and put away, we determined that I was in good enough shape to make the trek back over to Tiger's Eye. Mama B felt my face for fever and Rachel took my pulse.

"I'm fine. I'm fine," I said, waving them away. I felt stronger than I had in days, even with an occasional twinge from my run-in with the wild pig. And the Bonapartes had a grieving young woman in the house. They didn't need a bunch of strangers underfoot.

Baby, though, elected to stay behind to help out Earl and Sharelle. She told us that she'd miss supper but that she would be back later in the evening. As she kissed me on the cheek, I felt guilty for calling her out about her propensity to wear nearly no clothes. That had been small of me, and she had pushed back, rather properly, I thought. In fact, all afternoon she'd behaved as though she were a poster child for maturity, as if this family were her ballast.

Mama B gave me salve for the wound and tea for the nausea. When we left, Barbara on one side of me and Rachel on the other, Mama B hugged each of us and then said to me, "You tell Mac I love him and that he best come see me. And you, missy"—she planted a kiss on my forehead—"take care of that child growing inside you. What a precious gift!"

"Yes, ma'am, I will. I promise." Next to my wedding vows, it was the most solemn pledge I'd ever made.

*   *   *

That night, under clear skies, we were treated to a most amazing meteor shower. Enchanted, Barbara, Rachel, and I gathered at the water's edge, lolled in the surf, and watched stars streak across the sky even as the waves, building under the breath of another offshore thunderstorm, licked our legs. The saltwater made my pig wound, as we'd taken to calling it, tingle. But that was a small price to pay. The night air was sweet in our nostrils, the ghost crabs danced in the sandy distance, and above us the stars rained down. I felt blessed.

With the exception of the occasional "Whooooa!" or "Oooooo!" we were silent, wrapped in the night's glory, the three of us letting our minds wander as they would. I had actually closed my eyes, content to listen to the surf that reflected both the star- and moonlight, when Barbara said, so quietly her voice might have been part of the sea's whisper, "I've left Hugh. He's got an apartment. I'm keeping the house. At least for now."

For more than a ringing minute, I doubted what we had just heard. In fact, I was playing it over in my head, trying to convince myself that the wind was playing tricks, when Rachel, as usual, cut to the chase. "Are you going to be all right with it, Babs?"

"Yes," she said. "It's just that I don't really seem to know who I am anymore."

"You want to talk about it?" I asked, fear and sorrow weighting my words with heaviness. What a singular day it had been: full of discoveries, but this particular one in no way brought joy.

"Not right now."

My impulse was to cajole her into spilling it all out, but would that do more harm than good? Should we let her keep it inside, where it might fester and burst? With her dead voice blocking out the surf song, I feared that life was changing so quickly that none of us really knew the others anymore. Perhaps the years were turning us into strangers.

But then the sky full of star glitter bloomed over us again, and I thought, *At least I know where I am. I'm in a warm ocean on a green island with stars falling all around me. Maybe that's enough to start with. And I know that now there'll be another of me, whoever I am.*

Why was I so certain, without any medical evidence, that Rachel's nurse voodoo and Mama B's inner vision were accurate?

"Just because," I whispered.

"What?" Rachel asked.

"Nothing."

I pushed up on one elbow. The pig wound pulsed, but not so much with pain; it just let me know it was there.

"Listen, Barbara, you've got to talk to us. In fact, you've held it in way too long." Now I thought I knew why she'd taken to the bottle with such dedication.

"I think . . . I think I haven't said anything because I don't know how to talk about it. I mean, we've been married since I was twenty-two years old. He's the only man I've ever—you know—lain down with. The only one. It's like, I don't know how to breathe without him."

Rachel let out a heavy sigh.

"Who is it?"

A star fell, its trail so long and vivid, I thought it might splash into the ocean. In fact, I wanted it to. I also thought that Barbara might not answer. But finally, she cleared her throat and began to speak in the same lifeless voice.

"That new nurse. The one he hired six months ago. The one who is twenty-six years old to his forty-five and has the two-foot blonde extensions."

"Jesus," I said, "shades of Baby." First Teddy. Now Hugh. I felt my heart clench at the possibility of Mac's ever leaving me. Especially now.

"Yeah. But Teddy was single when he cradle-robbed," Rachel said. And then, "How'd you find out?"

Barbara's bitter laugh cut through the wind like acid. "Our annual Fourth of July party."

"What?" I looked at her, not fully believing Hugh could stoop to that. "In your own house?"

"Actually," she said, staring past us, "it's worse than that. Steven caught them."

"Steven!"

I didn't have to look; I knew Rachel's eyes were flashing thunderhead blue as she said Barbara's youngest child's name. And I also knew that eighteen-year-old Steven, who worshipped the ground his father walked on and was on track to go to premed at Vandy, was without a doubt devastated.

"Yes. He walked in on them in Kate's old room."

"Where the hell was everybody else while this was going on?" Rachel asked.

"The pool. Steven went looking for his dad because he'd left the burgers on the grill. They were burning. I swear to God, I can still smell them." Barbara closed her eyes.

Rachel and I remained quiet. It was as if we both sensed that after keeping this secret for so long, now that she was talking about it, the flood hadn't yet abated. A night bird skimmed the water, disappeared in the darkness.

"Steven knew something was probably wrong with a patient. Indigestion. Finger cut. A burn. Somebody in crisis. Who could have imagined that his father had simply decided to grab a quickie in his daughter's bedroom?"

Barbara's voice thickened and this time I knew it wasn't alcohol coating her words, but tears and disbelief.

"Son of a bitch!" Rachel sat up and glared into the distance.

"What are you going to do, Babs?"

Barbara sighed again, as if this new world were too much for her.

"I have no idea. With Steven leaving for Vandy, I will be completely alone. And angry. No matter what, no matter what I say or do or think about, I am angry. I feel like it's burning me alive."

"Take him to the cleaners, girl," Rachel said. "Nail it down."

"That's not going to be a problem," Barbara said. "But I don't know if the kids are ever going to speak to him again."

"Well," I said, staring at the sky, an odd mix of sadness and elation over what I thought my new life might become surging through me, "I hope he finds a way to win them back. Although right now I don't think he deserves it."

"Neither do I," she said matter-of-factly. "And in

the meantime, I have ten more pounds to lose and I'm seeing a personal trainer. Hugh might be screwing someone young enough to be his daughter, but I'm not going to just roll over. I'm going to figure out who the hell I am and look damn fine while I'm doing it."

"Hear, hear!" Rachel said. She scrambled to her feet, filled our wineglasses, mine with fizzy water, before returning to her spot in the ruffled surf's edge. "The future is one hell of an uncertain place. But let's drink to it anyway."

Dark guilt swirled through me. My life was suddenly all roses. But not Barbara's and surely not Rachel's.

"If you need anything at all, Babs, you let me know." And then I slipped up and said. "You too, Rach. The minute anything comes up."

Rachel didn't respond, but after a brief pause, Barbara asked, "Why would Rachel need your help?"

I wanted to run. I wanted to cry. I wanted to scream. I wanted the fucking universe to be a kinder place. Not only had I almost gone back on my promise to my friend not to tell anyone about her illness, but because I'd brought it up, Rachel's cancer was real again. Alive and bouncing like a hot red orb circling the three of us. But Rachel saved me.

"I don't," she said. "Maddy's just being nice."

"I see," Barbara said quietly, and there was something about her tone—her quick acceptance—that made me think she didn't believe Rachel. But she let it go. This was our time together, our magic August. And it was almost over. Just a few more days and we'd be off this island and back to our real lives and our real sorrows, and our real and hard-won joys.

So the three of us, content to try to make the best of the time we had left together, stargazed in silence. Eventually the meteor shower faded to black and we were left with the ordinary stars, the ones that were fixed and eternal.

"I think," Rachel said finally, rising and stretching her arms overhead, "we should build a fire…"

"And toast some marshmallows!" Barbara said.

"I'll go get them," I said, struggling to get to my feet.

"Oh no you don't, Miz Pig Wound," Rachel said, helping me up. "You stay out here and off that leg." She looked down the beach. "Who knows? Maybe Baby will show up."

"At least we know what's going on now," I said. "Earl and Mama B are really nice people. I hope I get to meet the rest of the family one day."

"Shame about his baby," Barbara said. She put her arm around me. "Don't worry, Maddy. You and yours are going to be just fine."

"I don't even know for sure," I said, but I couldn't suppress my grin. And then I said, rubbing my belly—I so wanted to have a bump—"I wish Baby would get back here. I mean, it's lovely that she's over there helping out and whatnot, but she shouldn't be coming in so late at night."

"What could happen to her on this little island?" Rachel asked.

"She could drown. She could fall and break something," I said.

Barbara said, the delight returning to her voice, "Can you imagine one of those tits broken?"

"Wild pigs. We know they can hurt you," I said.

"Ah, yes," Rachel said, heading up to the house. "Can't you just see a terrified herd of pink piggies fleeing before those boobs?"

We all laughed and Barbara pointed to the beach chairs that were just out of reach of the surf. "Sit. You need your rest."

And I did. It felt nice being looked after. Barbara made the fire and Rachel and I skewered the marshmallows. The flames crackled and popped and we all looked mythic, a bit enchanted in its glow.

"Wind's picking up," Barbara said, staring into the flames.

"Yep, looks like that storm might come ashore."

"They do every night. Almost," I said.

We poked our skewered marshmallows into the fire and when we could see the sugar starting to caramelize, we feasted. The creamy, slightly burned sweetness tasted like childhood. I downed three in a row. I still felt uneasy about Baby's absence. Especially with wild pigs on the loose and a storm brewing. I was just about to say maybe we should go look for her, when we heard her call.

"Hi, ya'll! Is dinner over?"

She stood at the end of the beach, her near-nakedness shining in the gathering dark, her cover-up slung over one bare shoulder. But I couldn't judge. We were in our bathing suits too, except ours covered a whole lot more skin. Maybe, I thought, it was just a generational thing. Overhead, more thunderclouds were massing against the sky, and lightning forked from them, like the Devil tonguing the water.

"What are you doing down there?" Rachel called, clearly annoyed. "Get over here. We promised Teddy we'd look after you. Remember?"

"Oh, Teddy!" Baby giggled. But she trudged down the beach and joined us. "Oooo! Marshmallows!" She reached for a skewer.

"How's Sharelle?" I asked.

Baby settled into her chair. "She's OK. She was actually talking tonight."

"Maybe she needs a shrink," Rachel said.

"Nuh-uh. She just needs Earl." Baby scrunched up her face, appearing lost in thought, and then, as if she'd decided she'd had enough tragedy for one night, said, "Hey! Why don't we have a campfire sing-along? You know, belt out those old songs you're supposed to sing around fires. Teddy taught me all of them."

"What songs?" Rachel asked, her disgust for the idea evident.

"You know. Like, 'Roll your leg over the man in the moon.' And 'The admiral's daughter lives down by the water and she wants to steal your dinghy.'"

"Not on your sweet life," Rachel said.

"Besides," said Barbara, "it's fixin' to pour." She looked out at the ocean. "That storm means business."

"It can't pour before I toast me some marshmallows," Baby said, sticking her skewer into the flames.

"You'd better hurry," I said, sticking mine back into the fire as well.

Baby ate hers as if she hadn't eaten in a month. She licked the sweet sticky stuff off of her fingers. "Mmmmmmm! Now come on, let's sing!"

I was about to say that I couldn't carry a tune in a tin cup, nor did I feel like warbling old college songs, when the sky opened up. The fire sizzled and went dark. Thunder bellowed and lightning struck so close the flash momentarily blinded us. Barbara screamed and ran for the house. Baby laughed with glee and followed her inside. Rachel walked with me, her arm around my shoulders. We walked as quickly as we could, and I couldn't help but flash back to the night she'd considered ending it all.

"You stay with us, Rachel. You hear me?" I said as we gained the front porch steps.

But she didn't respond to my question. She simply said, "Quick, quick. We've got to get inside."

*   *   *

We looked like a quartet of drowned rats, but Baby, her long blonde hair matted against her breasts, looked particularly pathetic.

"Oooo," she said, shivering, "I've got to dry off and get into some clothes."

"Wonders never cease," Rachel said, heading up the stairs. "Where's Barbara?"

"Changing into her jammies, I think," Baby said.

"That," I said, shivering, "sounds like a plan."

We all retreated to our rooms. As I stripped down and dried off, the rain stuttered more heavily against the metal roof and a dankness suffused the house as if it might rain forever and ever and ever.

I pulled my nightgown over my head, grabbed the towel I'd thrown across the vanity chair, and wrapped my wet hair in it. I looked like a sodden scarecrow but didn't care. I thought about all that had transpired during our time on Tiger Island . . . Baby had been embroiled in a tragedy taking place on the other side of the island and had elected to act mysterious about her comings and goings without any good reason. Rachel

was facing a death sentence and had at one point almost decided to take fate into her own hands. Poor
Barbara had been dumped by Hugh and was drinking
her sorrows away. And me? I just might be with child
and an owner of some prime island real estate. *If this
isn't the ultimate girls of August reunion*, I thought,
heading out into the hall to check on everyone, *I don't
know what is*.

Baby's door was open. I stuck my head in. She had
changed into a pair of pajamas that had images of
Donald Duck all over them. She was belly-down and
sound asleep, and I imagined that at any moment she
might start sucking her thumb.

I went down the hall to Barbara's room. Her door too
was wide open. A half bottle of Cabernet sat uncorked
on her dresser, but she was nowhere to be seen.

Rachel's door was closed. The drone of her hair
dryer competed with the lashing of the rain. The
knowledge that she was inside the house, safe, shel-
tered from the storm, gave me a sense of relief. I
headed downstairs, keeping a tight grip on the rail,
step by step.

I went into the kitchen and poured a glass of water
from the refrigerator pitcher and then went in search
of Barbara. I called her name. Nothing. I looked in all
the rooms, finally finding her in the sunroom, where
she sat pondering the jigsaw puzzle.

"Aha!" she said, pushing a piece into place.

"Mind if I join you?"

"Not at all." She tried to fit a three-sided piece into the sky but it didn't work. "What's everybody else doing?"

"Baby's sound asleep and Rachel is drying her hair."

I found the piece that Barbara had been searching for and locked it in. "Bingo."

"Maddy?" She searched the loose puzzle bits, running her fingers over them.

"What?"

"Thanks for making me talk tonight." She found three pieces that fit together and placed them inside the puzzle, underneath the sky. They looked like hair and a forehead. "I feel better."

I almost said something about the drinking, but decided against it. She was a big girl. And she was as smart as they come. I had no doubt she'd get through this without my pointing out something that might only make her feel worse. And, I noticed, liquor was nowhere in sight; she was drinking a Diet Coke. *It's a start*, I thought, *and a good one*.

I returned my focus to the puzzle. A three-tabbed blue piece with a flourish of white: I found its place, and a light-bulb went off in my mind. "Barbara, this isn't all sky. See right here? That's ocean."

Barbara leaned in, squinted at where I was pointing. "Huh! You're right again, Maddy."

I still had no idea what the puzzle picture added up to, and I was tempted to try to find the box it had come in but decided that would be too much trouble. Knowing Baby, she'd probably burned it.

We worked the puzzle in silence for a while, enveloped in the sound of the storm, which showed no signs of abating. As the puzzle's elements began to fall together, we worked more quickly, our hands hovering over loose pieces, sometimes turning them over and over as we felt their crazy edges, sometimes holding them to the light as if by studying them more closely we could see their proper places.

Someone came onto the porch. I turned around. Rachel was in her silk jammies, her deep-chestnut hair newly blow-dried and glamorous. It was difficult for me to believe that she was as sick as she had been told.

"Wow! You look great," I said.

"A good soaking rain does wonders for the skin," she said. She lifted a mug of hot chocolate to her lips and sipped; it smelled heavenly. Then she pulled up a chair, but before sitting down, she stared down at the puzzle.

"Hmm! Well, I'll be damned!"

"What?" I glanced up at her.

"Look!"

"What are you talking about?" Barbara asked, trying to fit a piece with one straight side in the wrong place.

"I think that's us."

I looked at the puzzle, trying to see what Rachel saw.

"That photo of you, Barbara, Melinda, and me— the one you keep on your fireplace mantel—that's it."

"Oh my," Barbara said. "I think you're right. Look at this, Maddy. Right here. The chair."

Off to the left side, at about where the water began, was an incomplete image of a lavender Adirondack chair with the back shaped like a dolphin. There was only one place that had such a chair. The St. Teresa house. Our last August together. "Oh my God," I said. "It *is* us. It's Melinda! But how…"

"Baby must have stolen the photo when she was at your house. And then she took it to one of those photo places that turn pictures into puzzles."

"Why would she do such a thing?"

"Beats me," Barbara said. "Despite her lip service on the subject, she gets testy every time the subject of Melinda comes up, as if she wishes the woman had never been born."

"What do you think, Rachel?"

"I think she's just plumb-assed crazy."

Knowing what the puzzle depicted, the three of us quickly went to work, a new confidence informing our choices. As Melinda's face emerged, a lump formed in my throat. For a brief, somehow terrible moment, it felt as if we were resurrecting her.

"She's with us," I whispered. "I know it."

"No. No she's not," Barbara said. "It doesn't work that way."

Rachel did the final honors. She put the final jig-saw piece in place: a tendril of Melinda's hair blowing wild in the breeze.

"Wow," I said. There we were, the girls of August, younger, largely untouched, without a real care in the world. Not yet, anyway.

"We look happy."

"We sure do," Barbara said.

"Do you think she knew?" Rachel asked.

"Knew what?" Barbara flattened out the puzzle's left side, which had buckled.

"That she was going to die."

"She had no idea," I said.

"No one really thinks they're going to die," Barbara said.

Stone-faced, Rachel looked first at me, then at Barbara. "No, I suppose not." She kissed her fingertips and touched Melinda's face.

I put my hand on her shoulder, but she jerked away. "Don't, Maddy. Just...don't."

CHAPTER

7

Before sleep that night, I went on one of what Mac calls my dreamtime walkabouts. I've had these nocturnal odysseys often, two or three times a month, ever since I can remember. They aren't dreams; they haven't the luminous, shifting landscapes of dreams, nor their sheer Daliesque particularity. Mine all involve places I know or know of; the cast is always made up of people I know or have known, though once I had a long series of dreamtime escapades involving a black poodle we had never owned and so far have not acquired. I sighed and twisted comfortably into my accustomed sleep trough, and turned my head into the pillow so I could hear with one ear the lullaby of rain on the tin roof. What made it so utterly soothing? I could not remember having heard it often, and of course millions of children never did, and yet I was certain it had the lulling power of a mother's voice, or the tinkle of a nursery tune.

Under the rain I heard the voice of my cousin Jim Creighton when he was maybe eight or nine. Jim-Jim, as he was called, was adorably red-curled and copper-freckled, and a born menace. He had tortured his sister Francie and me since he could toddle...or scuttle, which was a more suitable term. He had frogged us, tripped us, shot us with his slingshot, decapitated our dolls, put gum in our hair, and once striped my white spitz dog with red paint. He denied all his mayhem, his blue eyes swimming with tears.

"They did it," he would quaver to our grand-mother, at whose farm we spent great chunks of summer. Grammy thought, as Francie put it, that the sun rose and set in Jim-Jim's ass, so she and I shared considerable punishment that should have been Jim-Jim's.

One day we couldn't really bear it anymore. I forget what this particular injustice was, but I remember precisely the red rage I felt rise in my throat. It was quite a mature rage, heedless of retribution. I could tell by her outthrust chin and flaring nostrils that Francie felt it too.

It did not take us long to decide. Jim-Jim's red Flexible Flyer, which we were never allowed to touch, leaned against the back steps. My grandparents' flock of Rhode Island Red and Dominecker chickens, who were shut in the henhouse at night, roamed free in the daytime, and left their splats of black-and-white manure everywhere. I wonder if any children of this time know the cool, slimy, dreadful feeling of chicken shit between their toes?

Jim-Jim had gone into town with our grandfather. We looked at each other. Neither of us spoke. She grabbed the wagon and I grabbed a shovel from the shed, and in a few moments the Flexible Flyer groaned and wobbled under a malodorous load. Jim-Jim alighted from the truck just in time to see us push it off down the winding dirt road that led to the calf pasture. By the time it hit a pine tree halfway down and shot chicken shit into the air like a fetid Old Faithful, his bellows were drowning out the 2:20 p.m. Atlanta and West Point freight that roared by every afternoon, delivering farm-fresh whatever to the city.

Neither Francie nor I made a sound during our spanking. Instead we smiled secretly at each other. Jim-Jim wailed for two days and would never again use his wagon. He said it still smelled of chicken doo-doo. Grammy finally bought him another one, and threatened any girl-child who touched it with far worse than spanking...though neither of us could imagine what that might be. In my case it didn't matter.

Vengeance was ours.

I smiled...I could feel the smile in my cheek muscles...and into the next slot came the living room of the big old house in Buckhead where I grew up, not far off Peachtree Road in Atlanta. My father was a partner in the law firm that his father had founded and though we were not rich, we were what my mother might have called *substantial*. That I attended an Atlanta public high school instead of St. Augusta's, which largely served the female young of our zip code, was a testament more to my stubbornness than to our "unsuitability." I was determined to play girls' varsity softball. St. Gussie's had no team.

It was April of my senior year, a tender, undersea-green April. April was starred with white dogwood and wild honeysuckle on the wide, smooth green lawns of Buckhead. I've Apriled in quite a few places, but to me there is none lovelier than that four-square-mile paradise of real estate just off the lava flow of Peachtree Road.

I stood in the middle of our living room in a drift of hoop-skirted green tulle while my father sipped his evening Cutty and smoked his pipe and my mother, on a step stool, fiddled with my hair and cried.

I'd have cried too, except that it would have meant admitting that I had been wrong, and I would rather have been flayed alive. That afternoon, after a week-long running battle with my mother over cutting my hair, I had lopped it off myself and slicked it down with a virulent gel that smelled like the library paste of my childhood, the kind that we ate in spoonfuls. Instead of looking like Audrey Hepburn, I looked like Prince Charles just out of his royal shower.

"You cannot go looking like that," my mother said through clenched teeth. "What would Terry say?"

She hit a nerve there. Terry Stabler was the biggest BMOC at Pace High. He was handsome. He was built like a young Adonis. It was rumored that he had dated half the girls in north Atlanta and slept with most of those. His grades were good enough to slide him into Princeton the following fall, and he was the best linebacker the Pace Panthers had ever had. In fact, he had almost single-handedly pulverized the mighty Burbage Tigers in an exhibition game the night before. I had not seen it, but the Atlanta sports pages had featured it, and him.

No one, including me, was quite sure why he had asked me to the prom. But he had, and now I had ruined the whole thing with, as my mother snarled, pinking shears and a can of Crisco.

"I know," she cried suddenly, straightening up. "Where is your stole?"

"On my bed. Nobody wears stoles anyway..."

"Get it."

I did, and handed her the oblong of filmy green.

"Bend down here."

I did. I could feel her wrapping the stole around my head. I started to protest.

"Hush," she said. "I'm giving you a snood. Look up now..."

I did. I saw a pretty girl in green tulle with her hair wrapped in green like a loaf of bread.

"*Mother*..."

"Lean down here!"

More scrabbling at my head.

"*Now* look!"

I did. She had pinned the stole so that it stood up around my head like a sort of miter. Under it my Adam's apple bobbled furiously.

"You look stunning!"

"I look like a demented nun!"

"No, you..."

The doorbell rang. Silently my father got up and opened the door.

"Well good evening, Terry," he said cordially, as if two semi-hysterical women had not just been shrieking behind him. "You look mighty spiffy tonight."

Terry was splendid in his tuxedo. It was widely known that he owned his own.

"Thank you, sir," he said, and smiled.

My mother made a small, mouselike sound in her throat. I simply stared.

Terry's two front teeth were missing.

"Sorry about that." He beamed around at us with

the air of one who knows perfection cannot be damaged.

"I can't get an appointment till Monday. I've got one of 'em, but I think the other one is still stuck in the tight end's fist."

Oh, yes, we went to the prom. And oh, yes, my mother insisted that my father take a picture before we left. I don't remember the prom, but the picture has sat on Mac's desk for years. He loves it.

Still smiling there in the dark all those years later, I turned on my back and stared at the ceiling. Such spring-sweet, innocent times. So long ago. Long before now. Long before us.

Long before the girls of August.

Another April came now, this one much later. This one not yet lived. Soon, though, I thought, tears burning my eyes. An April to sear the heart, coming soon.

*　　　*　　　*

We buried Rachel in the spring, in fact, that next April. The dogwoods were blooming, turning the world into a snowfall of white petals. The soft breeze was fragrant with confederate jasmine, rose, wisteria, magnolia. If we had to do it, I thought as I watched Mac, Hugh, Teddy, and Rachel's brother lower her casket into the damp red earth, I was glad that it was in the spring, when life pulsed sweet and green.

By the grave, as mourners began to drop small lumps of earth on my friend's casket, the world blurred behind a haze of tears. I couldn't have told you who had been at the memorial service. I couldn't say with any clarity who was dropping earth. My mind was frozen in grief and loss. Mac caught me by the arm.

"Are you OK, baby?"

I could not speak.

"Let's get you out of here." He steered me beyond the gravesite to our car. Once we were in it, he held me tight and kissed my face.

My heart sank deep, broken in half under the weight of love.

In the close dark of Tiger's Eye I shook my head fiercely. No. No. The graveside slid away and Melinda came.

My dream was thronged with images of Melinda. Melinda on her wedding day, wearing a column of ivory silk. Melinda throwing Teddy a surprise birthday party. Melinda jogging down the beach, her mane swaying with each stride. Melinda putting her feet up on a patio table, winking at me, saying the girls of August owned the world.

Melinda's face gone still and white on an icy Kentucky night.

"I have to stop now," I said aloud, crying. "I want this to be over. I want to go to sleep."

Then Mac's face came, filling me completely.

"Honey, we're going to have a baby," I told him.
His smile lit the world.

"It's about time," he said.

And then I did sleep.

CHAPTER

8

Even in sleep, I knew that the storm was growing stronger. I could see against my closed lids the white swords of the lightning, hear the ghostly sizzle that it made just before stabbing the earth, hear the great war cries of thunder, closer and closer, until the whole cosmos seemed to battle at our very windows. I heard the lashing of the trees and the banshee keening of the ocean wind and the echoing booms of the surf that had been so sweet and gentle in our ears just hours earlier.

A particularly loud and prolonged clap of thunder shook the house, waking me fully. Barbara, in the sleep-stunned voice of a child, called out in the dark, "It won't get us, will it?"

"No," I whispered, not at all sure. "We've got a tin roof and a lightning rod," I called, loud enough for her to hear.

"Go back to sleep, y'all," Rachel growled. "It's been a long damn day."

From Baby's bed I heard nothing but little burbling, smacking noises.

I crossed my arms against my stomach and whispered to the baby I prayed I was carrying, "Don't be afraid. It's just a storm. I'm going to take care of you, little one."

Lying in the wild dark, I ran my hands across my pelvis. No bump. Not yet. I felt only my own hipbones. *Oh, my God, Mac,* I thought. *We did it. We really did it. If I'm dreaming this, I'm going to cut my throat.*

Eventually sleep took us all again. I don't know how long we slept, but it was still dark when a deep and prolonged rumble roared through the house, shaking the very timbers. And then came the great white crash.

We screamed and scrambled out of bed. We spilled into the hallway, frightened and confused. Cold, whipping water poured straight down on us. At first I thought I was in the grip of yet another nightmare, but when Barbara grabbed my arm and shouted, "We've got to find cover!" I knew that this was all too real.

I looked up. The roof was gone. I mean *gone*. Angry coiled clouds roiled above us, and blinding sabers of lightning struck all around as if intent on skewering us the same way we had skewered those marshmallows. Under the force of the wind, the house groaned, and I felt the floor begin to heave.

"We've got to get out of here!" I yelled.

Panic-stricken, we descended the stairs, and upon entering the living room, saw an even more frightening sight. Flames bloomed in the darkness behind us. The kitchen was on fire.

"We've got to put it out," I cried, breaking from the group.

"No!" Baby yelled. "No, no, no!"

Barbara grabbed my arm. "Keep going or we're all going to die. Now!"

We followed her through the living room, which was filling with smoke, pushed open the porch door despite the gale wind battering it, and finally, dazed, tumbled onto the cold, pocked beach.

There was no place to shelter. The forest behind us lashed almost horizontally. We fell to the ground and huddled alone, our arms covering our heads. The wind and rain hammered us. Everything—the trees, the ocean, the sky, the house—sounded as if it were a single howling wild beast, rabid with pain and violence.

Barbara yelled, "We've got to get help."

"No! Where would we get help? We just have to wait it out," I shouted, but the wind stole my words and suddenly there was Baby, crawling into my arms, shaking with sobs, her Donald Duck pajamas soaked to her skin.

"It's going to be OK, it's going to be OK," I said into her ear.

"Where's Rachel?" Barbara screamed. "My God, where is Rachel?" She rose to her feet and stumbled as she turned in a full circle.

"She was right behind me," Baby said. And then she wailed.

That horrible night when I found Rachel in the surf flashed into my mind. *"Just wanted to stop it before ..."*

"When was she right behind you, Baby?" I took her by the shoulders. "When?"

"In-in-in the house!"

I looked back toward the fire, and a new horror took hold. *She's not coming out*, I thought. My God. *She's not coming out!*

Fast as an eel, Baby was out of my arms and up the steps. I could not have held her. She was too nimble, too quick, too determined, too slickly wet.

"No, Baby!" Barbara and I yelled in unison. But she was gone, disappeared into the flames and smoke.

Barbara screamed, "No, no, no."

"I've got to go get them," I heard myself say.

"You can't. Please, Maddy, you *cannot*!"

I couldn't just let them die. I stared at the once gracious house. Flames tongued, long and furious, out of the shattered second-floor windows. They danced and curled in the wind, driven by the energy generated from their own heat.

We had, I realized, escaped with only seconds to spare. And now I had to go back in and get Rachel and Baby. Filled with new life myself, I had to show them the way to safety, to life. I pulled away from Barbara, and as I did, Baby burst from the side door. She stumbled down the steps. Through the smoke I saw that she was dragging Rachel behind her. Both of them were black with soot, crying and coughing.

Baby shoved Rachel into Barbara's arms and flew back into my own. I felt the fire's heat radiating from her shivering body. Her bones were sharp, a child's bones.

"It's OK, Baby, it's OK," I murmured once more. But I didn't believe my own words. How were we going to get out of the storm? What would we do next? What if this house burned the whole damned island down? What if we were forced into the sea? As my mind tumbled over itself, searching for something, anything that might save us, I shouted, "The flares! Where are the flares?"

It was days later that I realized a burning house was visible from farther away than flares.

Rachel uncurled herself from Barbara's grip and dashed toward the house.

"No, Rachel! Stop!" I screamed.

I held on to Baby as tightly as I could. We screamed at Rachel.

"They're just inside the door," she yelled back, and then she disappeared into the boiling smoke.

Barbara began her mantra once more. "No, no, no, no!"

I was sick with fear. I feared Rachel was lost to us. I feared she would grab the bucket of flares and they, having caught a tip of flame, would explode. I feared she simply would stay. I feared that in this tempest, we would all die. Right then, lightning struck the rod at the peak of the widow's walk, and the great cobalt-blue globe—this house's eternal eye—exploded. Shards of glass rained down and just then, Rachel ran out of the fire, bucket in hand, and back to where we huddled on the beach.

Baby began to wail harder. Her body was contorted as though she were racked from the inside out. She could barely catch her breath and, between her wails, she made huge heaving noises. I didn't know what to do. I shot a glance at Rachel and Barbara. "Help," I mouthed.

Rachel looked around, her eyes frantic and hollow, and saw my beach towel had been left on the back of my chair. Even though it was wet, at least it might warm Baby up a bit. We wrapped her in it and pulled it tight. And still she cried.

"There, there," I whispered. "Honey, you've still got this part of the island. And Teddy can get you another house built in no time."

"It's not the house!" Baby bawled. "I don't care about the damned house!"

"Well, sweetheart, what's the problem if it's not the goddamned house?" Rachel asked.

"If I just could have fit in with y'all I thought I could be like you," she sobbed, "but I'll never be one of you. Not ever, ever, ever! And that is all I've wanted since the day Teddy first told me about you. It's all *he* ever wanted me to be! But I don't *know* anything. You made that perfectly clear. I miss my mom. I miss my dad. I miss my sibs. And I thought with y'all, I'd maybe find another family. That's what Teddy said! But I don't know about your movies and you don't know about mine. And I don't know about menopause or ancient history. And I don't *have* anything. Nothing!"

"Is that why you stole that photo off my mantel? I mean, we love the puzzle, but..."

"I didn't steal it! Mac lent it to us. Teddy has already sent it back to him by now."

"That was real nice of you," Rachel said. "Really nice, Baby."

"Yes," Barbara said. "It touched us."

"Why are you still crying, sweetie?" I brushed her sopping wet hair out of her eyes. "What do you mean you don't have anything? Besides being cold and wet and half burned up, I mean? Look at all you've got," I said. I'd try anything to stop the desperate bawling.

"You're pretty as a picture. You've got this island. You've got Teddy. You've got..."

"No. I mean I don't have anything *wrong* with me!" she hiccupped.

I looked at Rachel and Barbara in utter confusion. Barbara shrugged. She didn't have a clue either. But Rachel stepped closer. She seemed intrigued.

"What are you talking about?" Rachel asked.

"I mean, you've got cancer. And Barbara's getting a divorce. And you," she said, nodding her head at me, "you've got...I don't know...you've got a pig wound *and* you're pregnant! Teddy says the thing he admires most about you all is the way you handle the crazy shit life throws at you. 'Those gals are indestructible,' he said."

"You've got *cancer*?" Barbara shrieked at Rachel.

"How'd you know?" Rachel hissed at Baby, hands on hips, and then she glared at me.

"I didn't tell her. I didn't tell a soul. Not even Barbara," I said hastily.

"Why didn't you tell me?" Barbara demanded, beginning to cry.

"Because I was sworn to secrecy!"

"Because it's stupid! Because it doesn't matter! Because it's my goddamned cancer!" Rachel yelled. She jabbed her finger in Baby's face. "Answer me!"

"I spied, OK? I saw you and Maddy out here and I snuck down and eavesdropped. I thought," Baby said, straightening her shoulders, "that I could help. But then it got to be crystal clear that I wasn't needed. Or wanted."

"Oh, for Christ's sake," Rachel said and she spun away, busying herself with the flares. Her jaw set, she took them out one by one and planted them in the sand.

Barbara said, "Are you going to be OK?"

"No!" Rachel spit. "I'm dying."

Barbara's face whitened, but I didn't have time for her right then.

"Baby, listen to me. The three of us have known each other for twenty years. You're not even twenty-five, and we've only known you a little while. You can't expect to waltz in and be—well, one of us. It just doesn't happen overnight."

"Damn it!" Rachel said.

She was fiddling with the matches that we'd stuck in the bottom of the pail. How, I wondered, did she think she was going to light a match in this mess? I heard the scrape of the match and then the beginning whump of the flares, and I thought, *Why the hell are we doing any of this? Surely Mama B or Earl or somebody on the other side of the island can see this. But why aren't they here? Maybe everybody in the whole freaking world is asleep.*

I tried to count the days on my fingers and was pretty sure Fossey Pearson was still MIA.

As I stood there trapped in my swirling thoughts, there came a muffled whoosh and then a long, ashy-smelling sigh that faded away slowly, slowly in the slackening rain. No boom of flame. No great leaping white light. Whoosh and then nothing.

"Shit!" Rachel said.

"See, Baby? The famous girls of August can't even light a goddamned flare," I said.

"I've behaved like a total idiot," she wept. "I have to stop."

Baby looked at the useless flares and then at the house, which was by then fully engulfed, and she began to laugh. She changed moods the way a stoplight changes colors.

"We are a sight!" she sputtered.

Rachel grunted and Barbara lifted a hand to the sky. "I think it's letting up, y'all," she said.

I tuned in to the storm once more. Indeed, the rain fell more lightly. The thunder still boomed but it sounded distant and hollow. I looked eastward. The only lightning I saw emanated from the dying storm as it approached the mainland.

Baby sagged into my arms and I felt her laughter in all my muscles. It felt needed, like air.

"That's one helluva bonfire," I said, watching the flames consume the house. "I guess it's better to laugh than cry."

Barbara went over to Rachel, took the matches out

of her hand, and hugged her. They didn't speak. They just held each other.

And then Baby broke away and ran to Barbara and Rachel. She flung her arms around them. Neither Rachel nor Barbara pulled away from her. And just like that, Baby became a part of them. These two women who so loved each other had allowed her in.

"Mama told me when I was little that I didn't have a brain in my head," she wept, "so I'd have to be really cute. But I'm sick of cute, and nobody else likes it except Teddy. And I *am* smart. That was the one thing my mama was wrong about. But she couldn't ever admit it. And I'm not gonna hide it anymore either!"

Looking at her perfect, sculpted body in the light of the fire, I thought that Teddy wouldn't care if she had the IQ of a manatee. But, of course, I did not say so.

With the world as we knew it fast being consumed by the burning house, I stumbled toward my friends, and as I did, far out on the dark sea, the throb of small engines began to drift toward us. From off the northern tip of the island, a deeper engine, fast and authoritative, rolled in, growling over the sound of falling timbers and snapping flames.

The Coast Guard...yes.

I closed my eyes and put my arms around the girls of August. All three of them were laughing. How could they find laughter, the will to keep going, in the face of tragedy? In the face of a broken family and broken vows and broken hearts and looming death? I didn't know.

But I joined in their laughter anyway.

We laughed with helpless abandon and we hung on tightly to each other, and I thought that perhaps the wet night wind picked up our laughter and carried it out to sea, to meet the engines that came to take us home.

About the Author

Anne Rivers Siddons is the author of eighteen *New York Times* bestselling novels, including *Burnt Mountain*, *Off Season*, *Sweetwater Creek*, *Islands*, *Nora Nora*, *Low Country*, *Up Island*, *Fault Lines*, *Downtown*, *Hill Towns*, *Colony*, *Outer Banks*, *King's Oak*, *Peachtree Road*, *Homeplace*, *Fox's Earth*, *The House Next Door*, and *Heartbreak Hotel*. She is also the author of a work of nonfiction, *John Chancellor Makes Me Cry*. She and her husband, Heyward, split their time between their home in Charleston, South Carolina, and Brooklin, Maine. For more information, you can visit www.AnneRiversSiddons.net.

Reading Group Guide

Discussion Questions

1. This novel focuses on female friendships. Do you have a group of friends like the girls of August? Is this type of relationship uniquely female? How do you think male friendship differs from female friendship?

2. The girls of August went to the beach every summer for fifteen years, even after their lives took them in different directions. Do you have any longstanding traditions with friends or family? If so, how have you maintained them over the years and through different stages of life?

3. Mac is adamant that he and Maddy should not do any fertility tests or treatments. He says that they are in this together and it's better there is "no one person to blame." Do you agree with him?

How does their inability to have children affect Maddy?

4. Baby is constantly being compared to Teddy's former wives, Melinda and Cornelia. Is this fair or unfair? Does this prevent the girls of August from getting to know her as an individual? Do you find it difficult to bridge age differences and form strong bonds with older and/or younger people?

5. Maddy is profoundly affected by her relationship with the young cancer patient, Tiffany Hodges. What does Tiffany represent to Maddy? Does she foreshadow some of the revelations that are uncovered later in the book?

6. Maddy has many dreams about Mac and their marriage over the course of the book. What is the significance of these dreams? What do they say about Mac and Maddy's relationship?

7. Food plays a big part in the day-to-day of a vacation with the girls of August. What importance does food have in your social gatherings?

8. Why doesn't Rachel tell her family about her illness? Is it fair for her to ask Maddy to keep her secret as well? Why do you think she runs into the ocean during the storm? Are there other ways that her diagnosis changes her behavior during the vacation?

9. Why does Baby hide her relationship with Earl

and Mama B from the other women? Does this affect the way the other women view her? How does the revelation of her secret change their opinion of her?

10. What does Hugh do that causes Barbara to leave him? How does the experience change her? Do you think that Hugh deserves to have his children forgive him?

11. What image does the puzzle show when it is completed? Why does Baby choose this image? What is its significance to the girls of August?

12. At the end of the book, Baby explains why she wanted to join the girls of August: "I thought with y'all, I'd maybe find another family." Do you have friends who have become a family to you?

13. How does this summer change each of the girls of August? Do you think they have become closer? Do you think Baby could eventually become fully integrated into and embraced by the group?